This book is due for ret

NO F

No Fear
LOW
823
HAL

005415

NO FEAR
SYLVIA HALL

SCHOLASTIC
PRESS

Scholastic Children's Books,
Commonwealth House, 1–19 New Oxford Street,
London, WC1A 1NU, UK
a division of Scholastic Ltd
London ~ New York ~ Toronto ~ Sydney ~ Auckland
Mexico City ~ New Delhi ~ Hong Kong

First published in the UK by Scholastic Ltd, 2001

Copyright © Sylvia Hall, 2001

ISBN 0 439 99860 3

All rights reserved

Typeset by M Rules
Printed by Cox and Wyman Ltd, Reading, Berks

10 9 8 7 6 5 4 3 2 1

The right of Sylvia Hall to be identified as the author of this work has been asserted by her in accordance with the Copyright, Designs and Patents Act, 1988.

This book is sold subject to the condition that it shall not, by way of trade or otherwise, be lent, resold, hired out, or otherwise circulated without the publisher's prior consent in any form of binding or cover other than that in which it is published and without a similar condition, including this condition, being imposed upon the subsequent purchaser.

*For Michael Menson – musician.
Who died on February 13, 1997, from injuries sustained when he was doused with petrol by white youths and set alight.*

*Thanks to Higham Writers, Danny Scott, Sam Genders,
Colin and Hannah.*

CHAPTER ONE

"We're not living here! Promise me!"

I dropped my suitcase, tottered forward on my platform shoes, and gulped.

All I could see were concrete tower blocks, grimy windows and rusting balconies; weeds sprouting from cracked paving slabs and litter whirling in dark corners. What a dump! I felt as if I'd been smacked in the face.

"Don't worry," Dad said. "We're round the back. These blocks are coming down soon."

I raised my eyebrows. "Brilliant. I've always wanted to live on a demolition site."

Mum patted my shoulder. "Come on. Not much further. You'll see."

And they set off again. Mum, tall and proud carrying an assortment of plastic bags like she'd just walked out the door of Harrods; Dad stooping badly but managing to look cheerful and elegant as he lugged a case that was even tattier and heavier than mine. And Patrick, my seven-year-old brother, whining all the way and carrying one little box of toys. I sighed as I hoisted my heavy load once more and staggered to catch up with them.

I hadn't wanted to move. I'd been quite happy in our spacious garden flat – almost perfectly happy. But then, a few months ago, two dreadful things happened. Dad had an accident and couldn't work and, as if that wasn't bad enough, just before Christmas, my lovely, precious Gran got ill and died.

Christmas came and went hardly noticed. We were like zombies. We ran out of money and when the landlord told us we had to get out, none of us had the strength to argue.

Now we were being rehoused on the other side of London – the Queensmead estate. A pleasant, safe area, the council said. Well, their idea of pleasant wasn't mine. This was urban jungle – concrete city: walls and pillars of chalky grey as far as I could see.

As we crossed a dismal open space, the concrete seemed to swallow us up, the blocks growing taller, the square wider. I gazed at the top of a multi-storey building that was nearly in the clouds. Perched up there you'd go mad, fluttering and squawking; scratching at the windows like a caged bird or vertically challenged battery hen.

Did people stay up there all day? There was certainly nobody about down here. It was empty, echoing . . . spooky. Where was everybody?

Then, from out of nowhere, three boys on bikes came racing towards us, grins wide as letter boxes. They rode straight at us, causing us all to stop suddenly; Mum lurching sideways into Dad, Patrick thumping up against Dad's back and me staggering into them all. The boys came closer, heading straight for us. Then, at the last moment, they swerved, before pedalling furiously away, their mocking laughter trailing behind them.

"Stupid idiots," I muttered.

Dad turned and gave me a wry smile. "No harm done. Just their way of having a bit of fun."

"Some fun if they'd knocked us over. Maniacs!"

"Cheer up, not far now," he said. "Past that row of shops, then under the bridge."

"It's much nicer over there. You'll see," Mum said, throwing me a bright smile.

I refrained from saying that it couldn't be much worse. With grim determination I picked up the damned suitcase again, hating myself for having worn platforms. God knows who I thought I'd impress – my feet were killing me.

I hobbled off towards the shops, stumbling slightly as I studied the glaring graffiti – ARSENAL and GUNNERS in blood red, loads of four-letter words and the usual Daz loves Shaz type stuff with hearts and crosses. And everywhere, red circles with the letter W inside, kind of like gang symbols or something.

On the slabbed forecourt in front of the shops, two women with pushchairs and a group of kids about my age stopped talking so they could have a good stare at us. Nobody spoke as we passed but I could tell what they were thinking. Can't afford a removal van – got to carry their own stuff and what they've got looks like rubbish. I suppose we looked like refugees fleeing from some terrible war.

To avoid the stares I fixed my eyes firmly on the bobbing curls of Mum's head in front of me. Suddenly, a swooping roller-blader cut through our ranks and thumped into Patrick's arm, knocking him off balance. All eyes swung towards him as he yelled and jiggled about like a puppet on a string before landing slap on the concrete. His box thumped down beside him, a corner burst open and precious soccer cards, a toy tank and soldiers spilled out.

Oh, sweet Jesus, don't let him cry, I prayed. Don't let him have one of his hysterical end-of-the-world tantrums, not here, not now. I gazed over people's heads, at the steamy windows of a launderette and tried to pretend I was miles away as Patrick sniffed and scrabbled about on the pavement trying to retrieve his cards. Then a movement caught my eye; a thin-faced lad stepped forward and placed a foot on one of Patrick's cards as it floated in a puddle. Just as Patrick reached for it the lad pressed it down into the muddy water. I glared at him – Patrick might be a pain, but those cards were his treasure.

Mum had seen too and she stepped towards the gangly lad. Quelling him with a look that would strip wallpaper, she bent gracefully to pick the muddy card from the puddle, then helped Patrick to his feet. Dad stooped to pick up the rest of the cards and I retrieved the soldiers and toy tank from the gutter. Not one of the spectators offered to help.

As Dad pushed the cards back into the box, Patrick's lip quivered and his eyes were luminous with tears.

Dad patted his head. "Don't worry, son. We've got them all. Soon dry them out when we reach home."

He handed the box back to Patrick. "Keep your hand on that corner, then they won't spill."

I heard muttering from the watching shoppers. "Who are they?" a girl asked.

I couldn't hear what her friend said, but it made them laugh. I turned and fired a look of pure hate in their direction.

"Thinks a lot of herself, don't she?" the girl said loudly, as we walked away.

Her eyes burnt into my back and my heart seemed to grow as heavy as my suitcase. I didn't like this place – new house or not.

Mum and Dad seemed oblivious though. "We're dancin', dancin' in the street," Mum sang jauntily, waving her hands despite her armful of carrier bags while Dad grinned, marching along by her side.

I lagged behind and by the time our path led us under the wide concrete bridge I was on my own. It was dark and gloomy under the bridge with an acrid smell of old pee pervading the dank air. Behind me I heard footsteps. When I stopped, so did they; someone was following me, but when I peered into the gloom nobody was there. I couldn't see where I was treading and caught my shoe in a pothole, the hard rim of the case jamming into my shin. I swore loudly and thought I heard stifled laughter.

I hurried on as fast as I could, skirting round puddles where water was dripping from the roof. Then suddenly I was out in the light, blinking, and in front of me, I saw a lone tree studded with pink blossom. It had appeared as if by magic and just at that moment, the sun broke through, turning it into a brilliant rosy cloud. A bird began to sing and my spirits lifted. Beyond the tree I saw a row of neat houses with shiny windows and tidy curtains.

"There it is," Dad shouted.

In the distance Mum waved. "Come on, Goldie. Look, it's that one . . . next to the end. See, the one with red railings."

I staggered towards them.

"Only a few steps more, we'll be inside and I'll make us a nice pot of tea," Mum said.

The others were practically running but I took my time, plonking my case down and having a good stare round. The house looked OK, just as Dad had promised, and the surroundings were better back here. New street lamps, neat brick walls, newly planted trees. A bit more hopeful than the concrete jungle behind me.

I turned and glanced back at the grey blocks; rows of windows glaring like eyes – some blocks twenty storeys high. We were lucky, there'd be nobody banging about on our ceiling.

Of course, Patrick had to spoil my moment of quiet contemplation by shouting loudly for me to hurry up. I was just about to stagger the last few steps when I became aware of a figure emerging from behind one of the pillars of the walkway. Had he been following me? Well, let him – so what! Nothing better to do in this place I supposed, and people would be curious about who was moving in.

I swung the suitcase sideways through the gate. Ouch! Suddenly my wrist gave way and I dropped it. Behind me I heard the boy snigger. I looked back. He'd moved closer and was staring at me. He strutted forward and stopped a few metres from the gate.

He was tall and lanky with a long, sharp nose and close-cropped blond hair. His mouth was set in a mean, hard line and his eyes glinted like splinters of blue steel as they swept over me. He coughed loudly. Was he going to say something – a word of welcome, perhaps? No. He coughed again, hacking deep into his throat, then he gurgled and spat. A big gob of phlegm landed in front of the gate almost at my feet.

I recoiled in horror, staring at the glistening globule. Then I lifted my eyes to his and was about to tell him how revolting he was, never mind about the threat to public hygiene, but Mum chose exactly that moment to shout down the path.

"Come on, Goldie. We've all got to go in together for good luck."

The lad's face wrinkled into a sarcastic sneer. I pulled myself up to my full height and gave him one of my "you're a turd beneath my feet" glares before I walked away.

"Thought we'd lost the key," Mum said, as I joined them at the front door. "Your Dad searched all his pockets . . . then I found it in my purse."

They were all looking pleased as punch – none of them had noticed our less than friendly neighbour.

Mum grabbed hold of my arm. "Goldie, concentrate. Now, we all go in together, then we say, 'bless this house' three times and turn around twice when we get inside."

Dad laughed. "What's this, Yvette? Some African nonsense?"

Mum laughed too, her brown eyes shining with mischief. "Maybe it is or maybe I jus' made it up. I think this house gonna be lucky for us. Come on, let's bless it."

I stood back as she put the key into the lock and turned. The door swung open and a smell of new paint sprang out at us. We hesitated a moment, then Mum spread out her arms, guiding Dad and Patrick inside and pulling me in after them.

"Bless this house, bless this house, bless this house," they chanted – me joining in on the third chorus.

Then Patrick dropped his box and began spinning round. "Why twice?" he shouted.

"For twice the good luck," gasped Mum, as she twirled round and nearly fell over his box.

"I'm dizzy," Patrick yelled.

"Well, stop. I said twice, not two thousand," Mum laughed.

I thought Mum was having us on. She liked to remind us about her African roots, but I spun round twice to be sociable. When we stopped twirling Dad caught Mum in his arms and kissed her.

"Should have carried you over the threshold," he joked.

Mum smiled wryly. "I should have carried you," she said. "You bag of bones."

Suddenly we were all silent, struck dumb by the echoing emptiness of the place. We left the luggage in the little hallway and walked into a bare white painted room. Bare walls, bare windows, bare concrete floor. It was quite warm outside but cold in here. I shivered, rubbing my aching wrist.

Mum strode purposefully to the window. "Oh, that sun shinin' to welcome us," she said. "Come and look, David. If that isn't the very spot for me flower tubs."

Dad and Patrick went to stand beside her.

She pointed into the little yard. "I'll have me some pansies and forget-me-nots and primroses and . . . a camellia . . . a deep pink camellia."

Dad put his arm round her. "We'll get one this afternoon. Go down the market."

Mum laughed and slapped him on the shoulder. "I'm dreamin' boy. Practicalities first. You got to go and help Carlo with the furniture. And we need curtains and carpets before flowers."

Dad hugged her tightly. "Well, a tray of pansies won't break the bank."

I pulled off my platforms and wriggled my toes; the floor was icy – blessed relief. I padded over to Mum and glanced out of the window. She slipped her arm through mine.

"Well, what do you think? Great to have our own place, eh?"

"Yes. It's nice," I said, trying to conjure up some enthusiasm.

"Come on, I'll show you the kitchen," she said.

It looked brand new. Freshly painted, lots of white cupboards and a shiny stainless-steel sink.

Mum was ecstatic. "Isn't this magic?" she asked, as she stroked the smooth surface of the worktops.

I said nothing. I didn't understand how she could look so pleased. OK, I knew we were lucky to have been given a house but it didn't compensate for us being uprooted. We'd had a home with Gran – if the stinking landlord hadn't decided to throw us out when she died.

"So what do you think?" Mum asked.

I looked at her eager face. "I think it sucks," I said. "I think it's a grotty house in a grotty place. The estate is a dump and the house gives me the creeps."

Mum's face crumpled. She put a hand over her eyes and gave a heavy sigh.

"I'm sorry, but you did ask me," I said, dashing from the room.

In the hallway I collided with Patrick who was bombing around like an aeroplane, his arms outstretched.

"Careful," Dad said, looking up from the box he was unpacking.

"I'm just going upstairs," I said. "My room's at the front, yeah?"

"Yes," Dad answered. "Better grab it before Patrick does."

I was aware of Mum watching from the kitchen doorway as I collected my case and shoes and thumped my way up the bare staircase. I felt bad for yelling at her. She was the one who should be sulking. She'd been evicted from the home she'd lived in for thirty years. But it had been my home too. I'd lived there since I was born and I hadn't wanted to leave.

Bumping along the landing I staggered into the front bedroom, dropped the case and looked round. Well, I had to admit, it wasn't bad. Light and airy – bigger than I'd expected. Ever since Patrick's birth I'd shared a room with him, so it would be great to have my own space. I could make it my private pad. Put a "NO ENTRY" sign on the door, lie on the bed and turn up the music. I'd certainly need sanctuary in this soulless place.

I closed the door now, then dragged my case across the floor and pushed it under the wide picture window. From below I heard Patrick shouting and Mum laughing. I was relieved to know Mum had got over my outburst – I hadn't completely ruined her day.

Crouching down, I rested my arms on the suitcase, the sun warm on my back. It was quiet now, a complete absence of sound. In Gran's flat I was used to hearing traffic from the street; shouts of children playing. But here there was nothing – just a strange, empty, buzzing silence.

It was hard to imagine spending every day on this bleak estate, away from the hustle and bustle of shops and markets, away from all the people I knew, friends I'd grown up with. In fact, everything that had made up my happy life until Gran died.

I sighed, gripped the handle of the suitcase and gently tipped it on to its side. When I'd unfastened the catches and lifted the lid, my hand delved deep into the middle of my clothes, feeling around until I found something small and square and hard – the little silver frame that contained Gran's picture. There she was, wearing the straw hat with flowers that she always loved, smiling her broad, happy smile. I looked at the photo and remembered. Remembered every room in the flat, the wide bay-windowed sitting-room, the sunny hallway with its stained-glass windows, the high-ceilinged dining room and the warm kitchen where Gran waited every day when I came home from school.

"Now, how much learnin' you get in there today?" she'd ask, tapping my forehead, a smile crinkling the corners of her eyes.

It hurt to remember. No other place would ever seem like home. No other place would ever seem so safe and secure and so much a part of me. Sadly, I got up to set the photo on the window ledge. The sun sparkled on the silver frame but I turned it away from the light – I didn't want Gran's picture to fade.

Leaning my elbows on the sill, I looked out. Directly below was our own little square of concrete, fenced off by red railings. A little square of concrete – hardly fair exchange for the big lawn and masses of flowers and plants in Gran's back garden. And in front of our concrete square was more wasteland, a big expanse of concrete stretching up to the bridge which I could now see linked two opposite blocks of flats together. At least that lone tree, just in front of the bridge, made a splash of colour.

My eyes focused on the mass of pink blossom. Beneath it, petals whirled across the ground like confetti, blowing towards the bridge. Then I was aware of someone standing in front of one of the pillars. His back was to me but I recognized his clothes – it was the lad who'd spat so gallantly. What was he doing? He seemed to be bobbing up and down. Was he dancing? Surely not!

Suddenly he turned round and I was caught off guard. He saw me . . . and stared. Then he punched the air with a sort of triumphant gesture. Now, I saw what he'd been doing. Big red letters daubed the pillar. They were shaky, still wet, but the words were clear enough. I gripped the window ledge, my fingernails sinking into soft paint. I stared and stared, willing the letters to change, not wanting to read the message. But it was there, plain for all to see. My heart lurched as I read the words he'd sprayed:

BLACK BITCH OUT

And underneath that was the symbol:

CHAPTER TWO

I was still staring at the words painted on the pillar when Patrick came bounding into my room.

"You're supposed to knock," I yelled at him, rushing forward to push him out.

He stuck his foot in the door. "Mum said to tell you Carlo's here with the furniture. You got to come and help."

I pulled some trainers out of the suitcase and slithered my feet into them, glad of a diversion to take my mind off the big red letters that crawled across my eyes and whirled through my brain. BLACK BITCH. Why? Who? I looked down at my hands; like the rest of me, they were golden brown.

My fingers trembled as I fiddled with the laces of my trainers. I could still see the look of triumph on the boy's face when he knew I'd seen the graffiti. What kind of twisted mind did he possess? Just possibly no mind at all – a complete moron. I decided to stay well clear of him and turning my back to the window, I stood for a moment, hands clasped, breathing deeply, trying to calm myself before I went downstairs.

A sudden bellow of laughter gushed up through the floorboards and I recognized Carlo's deep husky voice. Despite my gloomy mood, I smiled. I liked Carlo and right now it was comforting to have him here; as if a bit of our old life had followed us.

I ran downstairs and into the kitchen. Carlo was talking to Mum, his broad shoulders and wide smile filling the room. As I darted forward to give him a hug, he caught me and lifted me off my feet.

"Hey, Goldie, my man. You taller and more beautiful than ever."

His beard prickled against my cheek as he spun me round and kissed me.

"I can't have grown, you only saw me yesterday," I laughed.

He set me gently back on my feet again. "Got yourself nicely set up here. Your Mum soon be queen of cuisine again."

I tapped his shoulder. "You're just hoping for some dinner."

"I surely am. Got to get my reward for all this hard work."

"I'm glad you're here," I said, smiling up at him.

The door banged back and Dad staggered in with a heavy box. "Hey, no standing around. Got to get moving," he urged.

I followed Carlo outside. He'd parked the van as close as he could but we still had to walk across a few metres of concrete then down six steps and along a narrow alley. This wasn't going to be easy work.

"Yo, Goldie. Go for it," Carlo said, as I picked up a heavy drawer and started for the house.

For the next half hour we were all busy trailing to and fro with drawers and boxes and chairs, puffing and panting and giving each other encouraging shouts as we passed. Even Patrick was doing his fair share.

A few curious kids gathered to watch us. "You gonna live 'ere?" "Where yer come from?" "What's in that box?"

Carlo gave answers that kept them amused but refused their offers of help.

A pale sharp-faced woman put her nose over the fence. I smiled and said "Hi", but she looked away. If she was our next-door neighbour she wasn't very friendly. Perhaps she hadn't heard me – she seemed absorbed in watching Dad and Carlo stagger up the path with a big wardrobe.

As I waited for them to pass, I heard her mutter, "Load of old junk."

What a miserable old bag! That wardrobe might look like a load of old junk but it held precious memories for me. I used to hide in it when we were playing hide-and-seek, huddling between Gran's best Sunday suits and hats. Perhaps the woman had a house full of priceless antiques or modern designer furniture but somehow I doubted it. Who was she to turn her nose up at our wardrobe?

In the kitchen I helped Mum unpack dishes and cooking pots whilst Dad and Carlo tried to get the wardrobe upstairs.

"Think I should go and help?" Mum asked, looking anxious as we heard a particularly loud bang.

"No, Mum." I said. "Better leave them to it."

"Your Dad's back's not up to this."

"Stay there, I'll go."

But there was nothing I could do. The wardrobe was wedged on its side and they were pushing it along the landing. No room for me. I held my breath as I heard more banging and scraping but then Dad and Carlo came downstairs into the kitchen looking pleased with themselves.

"Well, the wardrobe's in place."

I rewarded them with a bright smile.

"Enough room for a gospel choir in that big ol' thing," Carlo quipped. He wiped the sweat from his brow. "Phew. It's thirsty work."

Mum ran a glass of water and held it out to him.

"Water!" Carlo scoffed. "This all I get for my trouble?"

Mum laughed. "Time for something stronger when you finished," she said.

I thought Dad looked tired out already. His skin was stretched tight and pale across his forehead and he was holding himself in a stiff awkward way, his back slightly bent, arms braced at his sides.

"Just a few bits and pieces left now," he said, with forced cheerfulness.

"I'll go and get those," I offered. "You sit down, have a rest."

I plodded down the steps and along the alley to where Carlo's fruit and veg van was parked. One little kid in an

Arsenal tracksuit had climbed inside and was doing a Teletubby impression, dancing over dust sheets and yellowed cabbage leaves.

"Get out," I ordered.

He jumped down, feet bouncing off the steel floor.

His mate was holding a curly-edged pasta spoon that he'd taken from one of our boxes.

I snatched it from him. "Give that here. Clear off!"

"Bog off, yer mean cow," he shouted and stuck two fingers up at me before running away.

I slid the spoon into the box, tucked a few things under my arm and pulled down the van door before turning and heading back towards the house. At the top of the steps I paused and adjusted my hold on the heavy box before stepping out into the open concrete space. A movement behind the pillars of the bridge caught my eye and as I watched, a boy on a skateboard glided one-footed in front of the bridge, then raced across the slabs in my direction. I blinked. He was one cool vision. Long, long chocolate legs beneath baggy shorts, orange T-shirt, sleek muscles, graceful arms, bobbing dreadlocks. Poetry in motion! I did a double take.

He spoke. "Hey, you movin' in?" he shouted, his voice deep, melodious . . . chocolate sauce.

"Yes," I replied, smiling my most luscious smile.

"Where?"

"Over there."

He stared at our house, the only one with its front door wide open. "Got ya, man," he said. "See ya."

I started to walk towards the house as elegantly as I could whilst carrying a heavy, dusty box. Damn! Why had I taken off my platform shoes?

"Hey man," he shouted after me. "Life too short ya know. Don't carry no heavy load."

I turned, ready to make a sharp reply but was disarmed by the flash of his broad smile. Resting my box on the wall, I watched as he scooted over the paving slabs towards a downward slope, saw the sun gleam on his legs, his calf muscles rippling. He executed a quick turn, his body lithe, arms outstretched for balance. I blinked my eyelids, fixing his image in my mind. My heart lifted as I watched him skate away. Hmm . . . this place might not be so bad, after all.

I was still dreaming when a voice close by made me jump.

"Here, let me take that, you look whacked."

I was surprised to find a woman with bright yellow hair standing right next to me.

"I'm Nancy from next door," she said.

She saw me glance at the sharp-faced woman who was still peering over the fence.

"I'm on the other side," she indicated. Then whispered, "Take no notice of 'er. Twisted old fruit."

Her laughter gurgled like a drain as she took the box from

me. Then she marched up our path, her shoulders broad as a table, her hips rolling like bowling balls.

"Right," she said, pausing in the doorway, "introduce me."

Soon the kitchen seemed full of people. We gathered round Gran's old oak table drinking tea, the adults laughing and chatting together like old friends.

"It's nice to be starting from scratch," Nancy was saying. "I wish I hadn't done my lounge pink. Looks like a bleedin' poodle parlour but I'm stuck with it now."

Mum didn't hold with swearing. We couldn't even say damn, but she didn't seem to mind Nancy's language. She was nodding and smiling.

"They all know me on this estate," Nancy continued. "It's not a bad place to live. Gone down a bit recently but there's still some decent folk." She paused, twisting a big sparkly ring round her finger. When she spoke again her voice was quieter.

"Mind you, there's some as'll comment, you bein' mixed race like. Should stick to their own kind – that sort of thing. But if you ignore 'em, they'll soon get used to you."

Well, she was certainly direct, I had to give her that. I wondered if she'd seen the graffiti on the pillar, wondered what Mum and Dad were thinking. I glanced at them and saw them exchanging anxious looks.

Then Dad cleared his throat. "All we want to do is live in peace," he said quietly. "We won't be upsetting anybody."

Nancy nodded. "I treat people as I find 'em," she said. "One of my best friends was from Jamaica. Do anyfin' for each other me and Pearl. Broke my 'eart when she moved away! Colour don't matter in friendship, do it?"

There was an awkward pause while we all glanced at each other. Carlo shifted sideways in his chair slopping his tea, Dad put his arm round Mum and Patrick picked at a scab on his elbow. I struggled with a million replies shooting through my head but said nothing.

Then Carlo came to our rescue by reaching over to pat Dad on the shoulder and saying in his loud, booming voice. "You couldn't have better neighbours than these folk. I can vouch for that. Lived next to them for ten years."

"I can believe it," Nancy said.

It was a simple statement but her voice was so warm and affectionate that somehow we all found ourselves smiling.

Mum looked up. "Like your friend Pearl, I'm from Jamaica . . . by way of Africa," she said.

"Well, you're very welcome, wherever you're from," Nancy replied, holding her cup aloft. "Here's to you and your new 'ome."

I looked around at the things Mum had unpacked: the huge teapot, dinner plates, vases; I recognized them all and pictured where they'd been in Gran's flat. I remembered Gran showing me the pattern on that tall vase, tracing the delicate birds and flowers with her fingers. I thought of the stories she used to tell, stories of another life in another land. If I concentrated I could still hear her rich musical voice. . .

"Goldie, Goldie. Nancy's asking you a question."

Mum was speaking to me. I looked blankly at her.

"You weren't listenin', were you?"

I shook my head.

"Nancy want to know if you would like to go round and meet her grand-daughter, Miranda. She goes to the same school you attendin'."

I wondered whether I did want to meet her grand-daughter. I'd rather choose my own friends, thank you, but as I didn't know one person at the new school I couldn't afford to be choosy.

"OK. Yeah, fine," I said.

Mum raised her eyebrows. I could tell she thought I hadn't been polite enough.

"Yes, thanks very much," I said.

"Come round after three," Nancy replied.

In the space of a few minutes everybody vanished. Carlo and Dad took the van to pick up the rest of the furniture, Nancy went off to the shops and Patrick disappeared upstairs to sort out his toys. I was looking forward to unpacking my box of treasures but I'd reckoned without Mum. She'd begun cleaning kitchen cupboards and just as I was about to make for the door she pushed a cloth into my hand.

"Here, help me. No use putting clean things into dirty cupboards," she said, as she dripped Ajax liquid on to her pan-scrubber.

"But Mum, I want to take my stuff up to my room."

"That can wait. You help me now. This kitchen gonna sparkle."

It was useless telling her the cupboards looked clean. I knew she wouldn't be satisfied until we'd scoured every corner. As I wiped the surfaces, I could hear Patrick jumping around upstairs, zooming from room to room.

"Tell him to stop, Mum," I urged. "The neighbours'll be complaining."

Mum picked up a clean cloth. "What you care about the neighbours in this grotty place?" she asked, pointedly.

I rubbed hard at an imaginary stain. I knew I'd upset her earlier, mouthing off about the estate, but what was I supposed to do . . . lie? I couldn't very well say it was lovely, could I?

Another loud thump came from above. "He sounds as if he's coming through the ceiling," I moaned.

Mum laughed. "It's just high spirits, Goldie. He enjoyin' havin' so much room to run about in."

"Well, he'd better not run into mine."

Irritably, I scrubbed at the formica shelf but I knew Mum was right, it was good to see Patrick acting like his old self again. He'd been so upset when Gran died and howled for hours when he knew we had to leave the flat.

Mum turned to wring her cloth in clean water. "When that van get back with me pots and cooker, I'm gonna fix us a proper meal."

Suddenly I found myself smiling. Mum was brilliant. If I was honest, this move was harder on her than any of us, yet she'd managed to keep cheerful. I went over to where she was bending to wash the tiles and leant against her back, resting my chin on her shoulder.

"It will be OK, Mum, won't it?" I asked.

She turned her head, nuzzling her cheek against mine. "Course it will. It just take time, that's all."

"I suppose so," I said grudgingly. "But I miss home so much and my friends and . . . all the people we know and . . . We will see them again won't we Mum?"

"As God's my witness. We'll go and visit, soon as we can," she said, patting my hair and kissing my cheek.

I went back to my cleaning in a better mood and when Mum started singing an old Stevie Wonder song – "Baby, Everything is All Right" – I joined in.

After I'd cleaned two more cupboards Mum said I could have a break, so I ran upstairs, anxious to see my own room again and make sure Patrick hadn't colonized it.

The sun was still pouring in through the window, making the bare floorboards glow a golden yellow. I zig-zagged across the floor in my best Janet Jackson style and picked up my box of treasures.

First, I unpacked my shells; some a soft creamy white,

others speckled brown, hard and shiny. They lay like secrets coiled and curled on the palm of my hand. I arranged them carefully on the window ledge in my room. Then I unwrapped a big abalone shell. The outside was a dull, knobbly brown, just like an ordinary stone. When you turned it over, though, the inside shimmered; iridescent, pearly pink and green, swirling and whirling like sea mist.

I'd written a poem when I was little, "The Song of the Sea Shell". I wanted to describe how mystical and beautiful and perfect shells were but I couldn't make the words work hard enough. I tried pretending I was a mermaid and singing it instead, but my friends laughed and told me that mermaids had long yellow hair and blue eyes and neat pink breasts covered by sea shells. I was sunk. I didn't have any of the requirements. My hair was long, but dark as liquorice; my eyes, nut brown, and I was so skinny I thought I'd never grow breasts. There was no spare skin – it was stretched tight as a drum across my thin ribbed chest.

Now I was fifteen. I'd got the breasts but I no longer cared about being a mermaid. My skin would always be the colour of coffee and I wanted to sing like Janet Jackson or Tina Turner, not like some Disney character.

I placed my abalone shell carefully on the window sill where it sparkled in the sunlight, and then unwrapped my singing trophy – a slab of frosted glass etched with a treble clef and musical notes. On the wooden base was a silver shield which read: *Awarded to Marigold Moon. Hallet Cup for Best Solo Performer under 15*.

I placed it beside the shells, remembering how thrilled I'd been when my name was announced in first place. Behind me the choir had whooped and applauded and I'd carried the trophy home in triumph. That was before Gran got ill; when Dad still had his job and we thought the flat would be our home for ever.

Things had certainly changed since then. I leant forward on the window sill and looked out at the sun dipping below the bridge. Would I ever get used to this place? Ever be able to call it home? Mum and Dad were putting on a brave face and Patrick seemed positively happy. But it made me feel uneasy.

A cold shudder gripped me as, with horrible fascination, my eyes were drawn downwards; seeking out the slogan painted on the pillar. BLACK BITCH OUT. But I searched in vain – the words had gone, they'd been painted out. All that remained was the giant red W. I stared at it until my eyes watered. Who'd blotted out the rest? Had the hard-looking lad come back and done it? Somehow I doubted that. He'd wanted me to see it – I remembered his triumphant smile. But somebody had gone to the trouble of painting over the words. Who?

When a movement near the pillar caught my eye, I thought I might see whoever was responsible or catch the mean-looking lad spraying another message, but it was

Nancy who came into view, hurrying along and chatting to a girl about my age. Miranda, I guessed. She looked all right – a bit on the heavy side, short blonde hair, jeans, denim jacket. She was carrying a shopping bag which I guessed was her Gran's because she held it away from her body as if she wasn't connected with it.

I watched them come closer. Nancy saw me, pointed and waved. Miranda looked up. She had a big bright smile on her face but when she saw me, just for a moment, I saw the smile flicker and fade.

CHAPTER THREE

If it hadn't been for Mum I don't think I'd have gone to meet Miranda. I was reluctant, wary. But Mum practically pushed me out the door.

"How you gonna make friends if you don't accept invitations?"

I went round to Nancy's, knocked and waited.

Miranda opened the door and gave me a tooth-raking smile. "Hi! I'm Miranda."

No hint of awkwardness; if she'd been shocked by my appearance before, she was hiding it now. I smiled back. "I'm Goldie – Goldie Moon."

"Goldie Moon – cute name. Come in."

I followed her into the lounge. Nancy was sitting on a pink velvet chair, her feet nestled in pink fluffy mules resting on a pink furry pouffe. In front of a gas fire lay a pink woolly rug and the walls were papered with pink stripes. I could see what she meant about a poodle parlour but the room made me think of fairgrounds – candy floss, sticks of rock and toffee apples.

It was a room that demanded your full attention. On every available surface stood china ornaments: bells and thimbles, angels and animals, lots of graceful women wearing crinoline dresses, and dogs, even a couple of pink poodles. I knew I ought to be trying to make conversation but I couldn't. The room was so full of stuff that I just had to stare. On every shelf and table top and ledge there were little statues.

"I bet you've never seen so many, 'ave yer? My little menagerie. Like a booth at a fairground, ain't it?" Nancy asked, as if reading my mind. "All my miniature friends." Her big horsey teeth flashed as she laughed. "I keep telling everybody, I don't want no more. I don't know where to put 'em."

"Oh, Gran, yer know yer like 'em," Miranda said.

"Maybe. But it's the dustin'. Sometimes I feel like throwing darts at 'em."

She leant forward and demonstrated, her plump arms wobbling, bangles jangling. Her big teeth flashed again, then she settled back and asked, "Now what are you two girls going to do? There's Cokes in the fridge if you want 'em."

Miranda grabbed me by the arm and pulled me into the kitchen. When she'd found the Cokes she motioned to me to sit down at the little kitchen table. The coke fizzed and Miranda's eyes widened with curiosity.

"Why did you come to live 'ere? 'Ave you got any bruvvers or sisters? Where did ya live before? How old are yer? Got a boyfriend?"

I answered some of the questions and Miranda gobbled up the answers like a greedy puppy. I felt a bit uncomfortable because she wanted to know so much about me. But then she reached across the table, grasped my arm and smiled.

"I can meet yer at school on Monday mornin' if yer like. Show yer where to go and everyfin'. It's a big school and it can be a bit frightenin' at first."

Her bright blue eyes bulged, reminding me of fish in a bowl. I moved back from her intense gaze but I was grateful for her offer. I hated the thought of arriving at school on Monday, not knowing anybody, looking lost and lonely and friendless. Now I had somebody to show me round.

"Thanks," I said.

"That's OK," she said. "You can be my friend."

Perhaps I shouldn't have told her so much, but I wanted to trust her and she was good at drawing you out. She asked what music I liked and before I knew it I was off on my favourite subject.

"When we lived at Blackheath, I sang in the church choir. We did gospel – four-part harmonies."

Miranda looked baffled. Then she asked, "'Ow do you sing four parts at once?"

It was then I decided she wasn't a soulmate.

"Well, there's sopranos and altos and trebles and bass," I explained.

Miranda looked blank.

"Each person sings different notes but they harmonize," I added.

A look of understanding dawned on her face. "Like door chimes?" she beamed.

"Yes," I said, smiling. I decided we'd probably gone as far as we could on music so I changed the subject. "Do you know the tall boy with dreads who rides his skateboard around?" I asked.

"Yeah, that's Josh. He's cool. He hangs around with the Mabbott mob but he's OK."

"Who're the Mabbott mob?" I asked.

"You'll find out. Best to keep clear of them. There's some right 'ard cases in that crowd. There's two gangs on this estate. Wraggy's lot – he operates round 'ere – and Mabbott runs the black kids."

I thought of the tough-looking lad, the graffiti artist. Was the red W for Wragg? Was he the leader? Better not ask – his words had been obliterated. Let them stay that way.

I sipped my Coke as Miranda continued. "Josh keeps in with 'em. You 'ave to, to survive. You'll be all right though. They'll be all right wiv you but you'll 'ave to decide whose side you're on."

"What do you mean?"

"Well, yer not really black but yer not white neiver, are yer?"

I looked at my pale brown skin. "Am I black?" I'd once asked Mum. She'd taken my hand. "Your skin isn't black. It's tawny, amber, toasted bread, brandy snaps, crunchy cornflakes, light brown ale." She'd laughed and pretended to eat and drink from my arm. But then she'd looked serious and said something I would always remember.

"It's not the colour of your skin that matters but what lies in your heart."

"I'm mixed parentage," I told Miranda.

"Yeah, I know," she said, staring right at me.

I shifted sideways in my chair, looked away, then turned back and met her gaze. "I don't think the colour of your skin matters," I said. "I'm me – Goldie colour."

"Yeah, OK, fair enough. It don't bovver me," Miranda said. But there was a look in her eyes that worried me.

From outside I heard a big bang and I jumped up to look out of the window. Dad and Carlo were trying to get our huge, lumpy settee through the little gate.

"It needs lifting," I heard Dad say as I shot outside.

"Let me help," I said, scrambling over the wall.

Miranda followed and we both grabbed a corner with Dad and Carlo at the other end. The old settee was really heavy but together we managed to lift it over the wall. Then we faced another problem – it wouldn't go through the door.

We pushed and pulled and shouted, Dad the loudest of all, because his thumb got trapped between the settee arm and the door frame. After a few minutes we managed to get half of the sofa inside but then it stuck. It wouldn't go round the hall corner into the sitting-room. We couldn't pull it out and we couldn't push it in.

"Hey man, you want some help?"

It was the skateboarder, Josh.

"Yes, please," I said.

Now there were five of us, lifting and pushing whilst Mum looked on from the kitchen window, her face divided between hysterical laughter and agonized despair.

"Well man, you gonna be the only house on this estate whose door is always open. If it wet, you sit inside," Josh said. "But if it dry, you sit outside – like a weather man in his little house. And today there's a sixty per cent chance of drizzle but, for now, it's bright and sunny so get out that suntan oil."

Josh was diving from one end of the settee to the other, sitting, arms folded, cross-legged, miming rubbing on suntan oil or holding up an umbrella, and Carlo was laughing so hard that he fell on to the settee too. And Mum, who doesn't hold with shouting in public, was yelling from the window, "Now, just you sort that thing out before it starts raining. You good for nothing stupid men."

I was a bit worried about what people would think. I mean, we'd only just moved in and we were causing a riot. The kids who'd watched us before were back and they'd been joined by three women. Then the sharp-faced biddy from next door came round the corner. She was carrying two bags of shopping and had a loaf of bread tucked under her arm. I saw her stare, take in the situation then sniff in a sort of disgusted way.

"Knew there'd be trouble," she shouted in the direction of the onlookers.

One of the women nodded but we didn't have time to

bother about them. Somehow we had to get the sofa in before dark. "Let's tip it up, prop it on its end," Dad suggested.

So that's what we did. Dad and Carlo went inside whilst Josh, Miranda and myself levered the sofa upright. Then we pushed and wriggled and eased it into the door-frame. And all at once, just as if it had been made for the door, the sofa slid in upright, with less than a centimetre to spare.

The kids on the pavement cheered as the sofa disappeared through two doors and into the sitting room.

"Cor, that was 'ard work," Miranda said. "I think I've broken a nail."

Josh laughed and clapped her on the back. "A small price to pay," he said. Then, raising a fist, he declared, "People power! Brothers, if we all pull together, we can win the world."

"Thanks," I panted. "Do you want to come in?"

He grinned and flexed his skinny arms. "No, gotta fly," he said, jumping on to his skateboard and scooting away across the concrete. I shouted my thanks and he turned and waved, executing a perfect circle, as his locks bobbed in a swinging black halo.

"He don't wanna hang around 'ere too long," Miranda said. "I'd better be off too. I'll see you Monday, eight-thirty outside the main gate."

While we staggered in with mattresses and bed frames, Mum was cooking, and the mouth-watering smells became almost too much to bear. Finally, the last box was carried in, and Mum announced dinner was ready. Dad and I collided as we rushed to wash our hands and laughed as we fought over one small hand-towel. Carlo stayed to eat with us and we all crammed round Gran's old oak table. I remembered how Gran always set food on the table with a flourish. She loved to cook.

"Thank the good Lord and eat up," she'd say. She cooked what she called proper food – "none of this fast-frozen nonsense." And she'd taught Mum lots of Caribbean recipes.

"Thank the Lord I cooked enough to feed an army," Mum said, as she heaped piles of creamy potatoes on to big blue and white plates.

I passed the plates round then sat down to eat. I was hungry. I'd been too sad to eat breakfast; sitting in the kitchen surrounded by boxes containing Gran's precious cooking things, the walls bare of paintings, the cluster of notes and photos gone from the fridge, and no fire in the stove. It had all seemed so unreal.

Now I tucked into Mum's chicken dinner and enjoyed it. After all the tension and upset of the last few months, I was glad the move was over. It wasn't a brilliant place; I didn't like the estate but at least the house was OK, and Mum and Dad were looking happier and more relaxed than I'd seen them for ages. They were laughing as Carlo told stories about his customers. One man, he said, always made him check the bananas for spiders.

"Man, he convinced there be a killer spider on the loose. Last time he had me emptying all the boxes, I told him, that spider die as soon as he breathe the cold, clammy London air. That spider, a tropical spider – it could not survive in London."

He illustrated his story with exaggerated gestures, and I found myself laughing with the others. But when it was time for Carlo to leave, I suddenly panicked. While he was with us I could imagine our old life hadn't quite disappeared, that we were still amongst our friends. I picked up his favourite baseball cap which was lying on the worktop and put it on my head.

"You can have this when you come back to visit," I told him.

Carlo tapped me on the head and pulled down the peak. "Don't need blackmailing to come back and visit friends."

Mum put her arms round him and hugged him. "Thank you for bringing our stuff over. It make the place much more like home." When she lifted her head from his shoulder her face was wet with tears. She sniffed. "You better get going, it's late."

Outside it was deserted and dark except for the strong glare of streetlights. I did my best to give Carlo a good send off, singing a sweet soul song as I jived along beside him. I was just about to do my throwing a baseball cap up in the air routine when Dad made a sort of snorting noise. I thought he was laughing at me and was going to tell him off but then I realized, he wasn't.

He'd stopped suddenly and had a horrified look on his face. I followed his stare and saw Carlo's van, parked in a glitter of glass. The windows were smashed and shards of glass covered the road, glinting in the light. When we got closer, I saw the sign on the back door – a big red circle with a jagged letter W inside it.

CHAPTER FOUR

Bright light glared through my eyelids. I turned my head away, seeking the comfort of darkness. Half-formed thoughts nagged at my brain. Something wasn't right. The light was strange, why was it so dazzling? Where was I? I listened for familiar sounds but heard nothing, just silence buzzing in my ears. I opened my eyes, saw the blinding white of the walls and remembered.

I was in my new room – bare walls, uncurtained windows – in our new house on the estate, at the back of all those towering blocks and concrete walls. And I was drowning. I clutched at my old eiderdown as memories of the previous day washed over me – sharp, jagged images of broken glass, scrawled red symbols, crooked smiles and hostile glares.

I was submerged by a hopeless, sinking feeling. This place was like a bog, sucking me under. We weren't wanted here. The message was clear, in the graffiti, the nasty comments from the next-door neighbour, the sneering kids, Carlo's smashed van. We were being warned.

I blinked and pressed my head into the pillow but couldn't get rid of the gloomy pictures. Mum's face, like a torn photograph, hope crinkling and curling and fading. All through us moving she'd put on a brave face, but when Dad told her Carlo's van had been smashed, she'd just wilted and cried.

I'd left Dad to comfort her. I wasn't much use – I was crying too. Carlo had been so nice; more concerned for us because we were upset than about his damaged van. "Don't worry," he'd kept saying as we cleared the broken glass off the seats. And when we'd finally made the van fit to drive, he set off with a smile. "Plenty of fresh air on the way home," he joked.

I could have hugged him. But when he disappeared round the corner I burst into tears. It wasn't fair, Carlo didn't deserve anything bad to happen to him. He'd spent all day helping us and then somebody had smashed up his van. It was horrible. How could we survive in a dump like this?

I rolled over and pushed my head into the pillow, trying to blank the bad things out, trying to imagine I was back in Gran's flat amongst friends. Carlo, next door; Chola, over the road; Mrs Winter at the launderette; Mr Ahmed at the corner shop; friends at school and in the choir and, best of all, Gran.

But it was no good, Gran was gone and everything was hopeless. My eyes were sore from crying and I couldn't rest. I might as well just get up and face reality. I couldn't go back to sleep and I certainly couldn't go back to Gran's flat.

When I went downstairs, I expected to find everyone depressed, but life was going on as normal. Dad was fixing a wall clock and Mum had just returned from the shop with groceries and a Sunday paper. She was emptying her shopping bag, bustling about the kitchen in her old grey mac. Without a second glance she handed me a loaf of bread.

"Here, open this and make some toast."

I ripped open the polythene wrapper, pulled out some brown slices and set them on the grill. Mum was a flurry of activity, opening cupboards, wiping up imaginary crumbs, putting plates on the table.

I stood by the window staring at two little girls who were walking arm in arm in the early morning sunshine. I thought about Gemma and Chola pausing outside our old flat on their way to church. No need to call for me now. The choir would sing without me. Tears sprang to my eyes. I couldn't imagine ever singing again, not in this place anyway – it had no soul.

There was a smell of burning and Mum hurried over to me.

"Come on, girl. I been out specially for that bread. Don't let it burn."

I wiped my eyes and sniffed.

"Isn't anybody going to mention last night?" I asked abruptly.

Mum glared at me and put her finger to her lips. Then she bent her head and hissed, "Ssh! We said nothin' to Patrick 'bout it."

I could see the logic in not telling Patrick. He'd gone to bed before Carlo left, no need for him to know. But surely somebody had to go and help poor Carlo sort out his van.

Mum glanced over at Patrick and Dad. Dad was absorbed in the back page of the newspaper and Patrick was ripping open a giant Cornflakes box.

"Your Dad's going over this afternoon. Don't worry, he'll help Carlo," she said quietly. Then she took the toast from the grill and scraped the burnt edges.

I sighed as I set some more slices to toast. I couldn't help worrying. Carlo couldn't run his shop without the van. Stupid, mindless, idiot vandals!

I gazed at the toasting bread almost willing it to blacken and burn but Mum came and snatched it away and steered me towards the table.

"Come on, girl. We want to eat it, not cremate it."

When we were all sitting down she poured out tea and smiled brightly.

"It a nice day. Warm already, sun shining. We ought to go and explore when we finish our chores."

"Good idea," Dad said vaguely – he was still reading.

Explore what, I wondered. Slabs of concrete? Types of litter? Study the graffiti? But I refrained from saying anything and anyway, Mum went nattering on.

"I ask already where the church is but I'm no wiser. Nobody round here go to church. I ask four people where the Scott Street Baptist is and they don't know. Not one of them. I ask, 'How long you live round 'ere?' And a man say,

'All me life'. Can you believe it? He live round 'ere all his life and not know where the church is."

"Amazing," I muttered.

"No need for sarcasm, Marigold," Mum shot back.

"Mum, I wasn't . . . well, not really. I mean about one per cent of the population goes to church so it's hardly likely you'll find a devout Baptist on Queensmead estate at nine o'clock on a Sunday morning."

"What's a devowed Baptist?" Patrick asked, milk gurgling from the corners of his mouth.

"It's what I would like to be if I can find the blessed church," Mum replied.

Dad looked up from the paper. "Devout means a devoted follower."

"Like me an' Arsenal?" Patrick asked, his face lighting up, his eyes taking on a red glow.

"Yes, I suppose so," Dad laughed. "Here, listen to this. Gunners on line to win the Double. Bergkamp's goal against Everton yesterday. . ."

"Will you not read the newspaper at the table, please," Mum moaned.

I ate a few mouthfuls of toast whilst Dad droned on about the soccer match, then, as soon as I'd finished eating, Mum thrust a big plastic bag at me.

"Launderette. Dad need a clean shirt for tomorrow – got to make a good impression on his first day – and you and Patrick need to look decent at your new school."

"Oh, Mum," I protested. "I wanted to wash my hair."
"Never mind that. Hair can wait, clothes can't."

I sighed. I knew it was no use arguing. "I need plenty of change," I said.

"Take some from my purse," Mum nodded towards the drawer.

I counted out some coins then picked up the bag of dirty washing and reluctantly set off. The prospect of spending a morning at the launderette did nothing to lift my spirits.

My feet dragged as I made my way towards the bridge. The sun was shining brightly but it just made everything look more shabby; showed up the filth. Even the bright, blossoming tree that had yesterday seemed a symbol of hope now seemed to mock me; it was too pink, too gaudy. And just behind it was the big, uneven red splodge where that disgusting yob had sprayed his nasty message. I scowled at the pillar and felt uneasy as I slipped into the gloom under the walkway.

I hurried through to the open space at the other side, just as a little kid on a tricycle came racing through the pillars, his mum hurrying to catch up. I watched him pedal furiously away, ignoring his mum's shouts.

As I walked, I looked up at the tower blocks directly ahead. Windows stretched from earth to sky, square grey eyes, watching. There must be hundreds of people living here, yet there were only a few people about.

An elderly couple dressed in clothes way past their Sunday best came out of a tall block of flats. They walked slowly, leaning against each other for support. Their hats were faded and battered, their faces crumpled and crinkled like punched dough. I said hello but they looked away and didn't answer.

I came to the end of our part of the estate, set my bag down and looked around. Mum had reminded me – "To the right, past the little park and it's in the square." She had a way of making things sound attractive. I imagined swings and slides, umbrellas, tables, a fountain.

The park was, of course, the scrubby bit of grass we'd passed yesterday, and the square consisted of a banana-coloured community centre, a bookies – barred and shuttered – a mini-market and the misted windows and peeling paintwork of the launderette. The buildings faced each other across a pond of concrete dappled with unsightly shrubs, shoals of litter and battered benches emblazoned with badges of love and four-letter words.

I hurried over to the launderette, hoping it wouldn't be too crowded. I hated waiting and I hated working out how to operate new machines. When Gran was ill I'd had it all down to a fine art – exact money for each machine, exact amount of soap powder, exact time it took for each cycle. Now I had to start all over again.

A wave of warm, moist air met me as I pushed open the door. Machines were whirring and swishing and the air was sweet with detergent. Two women sat, arms folded, deep in conversation while their washing went round. I pushed past the women to the end of the room, confidently opened the round fish-bowl door and shoved all my washing inside, then stood back to read the instructions.

"That one's broken, ducks," a voice shouted.

I turned to the two women. Yes, they were talking to me.

"Thanks," I muttered, taking out my washing and shoving it into the next machine.

I poured in just the right amount of soap powder then stood back again, money in hand. I was a pro at this game, I'd brought plenty of change with me. I slotted in a pound coin, a fifty, two twenty-pence pieces and pushed.

Nothing happened. "Can be awkward that one. Give it a thump," the woman advised.

Gingerly, I hit the machine where I thought it might hurt – in its money slot. Still nothing happened.

"Allow me," a voice behind me said.

I turned round and to my surprise there was Josh. Suddenly the gloom lifted and my heart danced as he grinned down at me. Stupid with joy, I watched as he thrust a long arm forward and hammered twice on top of the machine. There was an answering clink of dropping coins, the sound of gushing water and the machine clanked into action.

"Gotta treat it right," he said.

"Obviously," I replied.

He smiled. "How's the new abode?"

"We've had a few problems."

Josh frowned. "What kind o' problems?"

"Oh nothing, it's just a big change."

He nodded. "Not many people choose to come 'ere," he said, looking quizzically at me.

"We had some bad luck," I said. Then, quickly changing the subject, I asked, "How long does the washing take?"

"Twenty-two minutes, thirty-seven seconds. And it's lucky you got here now to beat the rush. Another hour and this place'll be buzzing. One launderette between three thousand and fifty-two people."

"That's diabolical."

"Yeah man, it's terrible. You just try feelin' for that sock you know is stuck on the roof of the drum and some hunky man in his underpants pushin' you aside saying, 'Let me stick my Levi's in 'ere'."

"I wish," I said and I found myself laughing.

Josh looked down and studied an electric-blue watch. "I got fourteen minutes and thirty-eight seconds to wait for mine. You wanna drink?"

I nodded.

"Come on then. Your washing be all right. Nobody can steal it while it's in the machine."

As I followed him into the mini-market next door, I started remembering all the good things that had happened yesterday. The laugh we'd had getting the sofa indoors, the friendliness of Nancy and Miranda and, most of all, meeting Josh.

I was feeling much happier as we squeezed into the shop, past shelves crammed with food and toiletries. A couple of kids said hello to Josh and an elderly woman smiled on seeing him and asked how his Dad was. He answered her politely, flashing her a charming smile. I was impressed.

Pulling back the door of the cooler, Josh chose a chocolate milkshake.

"Try one of these, they're good," he said.

I looked up at his deep brown eyes; his amazing lips. At that moment I would have been happy to try anything he recommended. Picking up a carton, I trotted after him to the till.

A tall, dark-haired lad in a crisp white shirt stood behind the counter grinning in our direction.

"Hey, Nazim, my man," Josh said, when he saw him. "What's cookin'?"

His friend had big, dark eyes that were brimming with excitement. "Got the new amp yesterday," he said.

Josh put his milkshake on the counter. "Excellent. Nazim, ma man, we're in business. On our way. No stopping us now. We gonna burn."

He and Josh laughed and slapped hands. I felt out of it – forgotten.

"Burn what?" I asked.

Josh turned round. "Sorry," he said, quickly, placing a hand on my shoulder. "Naz, this is Goldie. She just moved in."

"Welcome to the jungle," Nazim said.

"Oh, it ain't such a bad place," Josh chided.

Nazim raised his eyebrows. "No. It serves its purpose.

You know if you can survive 'ere, you can survive plague, pestilence and the general depravity of life in a war zone."

"Don't mind 'im – he supports Arsenal," Josh laughed.

"And we won yesterday," Nazim said, "Which is more than I can say. . ."

"Hey. I thought we was talking about the band," Josh said. Now I was alert, ears flapping. I'd heard a magic word.

"What band?" I asked.

But Nazim was laughing, carrying on the banter with Josh as if they hadn't heard me.

"Sore losers, Chelsea," he said. "You'll see Goldie, when you get to know him better. Don't be fooled by his charm."

"I want to know about the band," I said, my heart pumping with excitement."

"You play an instrument?" Josh asked.

I shook my head, wishing desperately that I did.

Nazim leant across the counter. "Josh is the greatest guitarist round these parts."

Josh laughed. "Sure, man, that's a real big compliment. Check out the competition."

"Well, now we got the amps we can get the band together," Nazim said. "All we need is a singer."

My heart was going into overdrive. I wanted to speak, but the words fluttered and stuck in my throat.

Josh clapped me on the shoulder. "I don't suppose you know anybody who can sing, do you?"

I looked at him, spellbound. Then I swallowed and, suddenly freed, my words rushed out, louder than I'd intended. "You bet," I cried. "You're looking at the ex-lead singer of Blackheath First Baptist Junior Gospel choir."

My voice filled the shop and I heard somebody titter. Josh raised his eyebrows and glanced at Naz.

"Hey man, our luck's in. We've got a ready-made star on our hands," Nazim said, stifling a grin.

I was livid. I thought they were making fun of me and I tossed back my long hair and looked at them through lowered lashes.

"Anna Mae Bullock began her career in the church choir, I'll have you know," I said with as much dignity as I could muster.

Josh smiled. "I bet you jus' fine, girl. If you interested we could give you a try."

My heart thudded. Interested? Just try and stop me. I was practically singing now. "Yeah, I'm interested," I said, trying to sound cool.

Josh pointed a finger at me, nearly touching the end of my nose. "OK, you're on," he said.

Nazim leaned over the counter. "Who's Anna Mae Bullock?" he whispered.

Josh and I looked at one another and smiled. "Tina Turner," we said in unison.

"Well, if you can sing like her, you're in," Nazim said.

"Just try me," I replied.

Josh turned to me and smiled encouragingly. I could tell he was on my side and I was glad. I needed an ally. I wasn't half as confident as I'd sounded. My heart was banging like a bass drum. Singing with a choir was one thing, but a band, on stage... I'd dreamt about it, but could I really cut it? Well, I'd soon find out.

Josh suggested we go and rescue our washing right away and then find Zoë, the Centre organizer, to ask for permission to rehearse in the Community Centre.

When we returned to the launderette more people had arrived and all washers were activated. Somebody had taken Josh's washing out of the dryer and piled it on to a bench. Socks, briefs and boxer shorts had spilt on to the floor. He raised his eyebrows, muttered something, then bent to gather it up, shoving it all into a big plastic bag. I took my washing from the machine and put it in a spare dryer and then we went out, me running after Josh as, bag in hand, he scooted over to the Centre on his skateboard. He waited for me, holding open the swing door, and as I passed him, he must have seen the anxious look on my face.

"You were serious, weren't you?" he asked. "You wanna do this?" My heart flapped like a wild thing. "Yes," I said, nodding emphatically.

Zoë was in her office, talking loudly on the telephone. Her red, spiked hair bobbed as she argued with somebody at the other end of the line. She sounded angry – her grey eyes stared into the distance and her red polished nails twisted the telephone cord.

"You promised . . . two weeks ago," she was saying in a thick accent. "It's not good enough. There's water all over the friggin' floor."

I could tell this was a woman to be reckoned with. Her eyes flashed on to us and she motioned us in.

"Well, I want you round 'ere first thing tomorrow. Do you understand?" she said, her voice climbing upward on the last word. I recognized the accent from TV: Liverpudlian – scouse.

"Right then, ten o'clock it is," she finished, and banged the receiver down. "That plumber – wouldn't trust him to empty a bucket."

I felt we'd come at a bad time but she smiled at Josh and pointed to a couple of chairs.

"Sit down."

Josh shook his head. "No, we OK. This is Goldie. She just moved to the estate. She wants to sing with the band. OK if we use the Centre to practise this afternoon?"

Zoë looked at me, smiled and nodded. "That's fine by me," she said. "Bingo starts at seven . . . as long as you're gone before then."

She stared at me and raised one carefully plucked eyebrow. "So it's an audition?" she asked.

"Yes . . . sort of," I said, hesitantly.

"Great," she said. Then she looked at Josh. "Does Tiger know about this?" she asked.

"No. 'Aven't seen him yet."

Zoë grinned. "Well, you'd betta tell him. Wanna use the phone?"

Josh pursed his lips and looked thoughtful. "No, it's OK. I'll go round and see him."

"Good luck," Zoë yelled after us as we left.

I wondered whether her words were meant for me or for Josh. I hadn't liked the warning note that crept into her voice when she mentioned Tiger. But I couldn't panic now. Things were looking up. I'd been given the chance to sing and I was sure as hell going to make the most of it.

CHAPTER FIVE

I was singing full throttle into the mike, twitching my shoulders, clicking my fingers, swaying my hips. I'd seen Tina Turner do it hundreds of times on video.

"A private dancer, dancer for money and any old music will do..."

There was no accompaniment – nobody knew how to play the song – but that didn't matter. I was used to singing acapella and in this fashion, I could really make the song my own.

Launching into the final phrase I stood still, held my head high and belted it out, giving it all I'd got. When I finished there was a moment's silence.

I peered through the lights, and saw Josh and Nazim as they began to clap and cheer.

"You dynamite, girl," Josh shouted. "You're knockout. Massive. Brixton Academy – here we come!"

He got up, came forward, clapped me on the back and shook my hand. He was grinning from ear to ear.

"You got the voice, girl," he said.

Then he slid round me, singing some of the phrases, "Private dancer, dancer for money," mimicking the way I'd moved, banging his hips into mine. I toppled sideways, then fell back against him and we were both laughing until we became aware of somebody standing impassively in front of us.

Josh immediately went quiet, straightened up and gesturing towards the person, introduced me.

"Tiger, this is Goldie."

Tiger was small and wiry, but there was something very determined about the set of his shoulders and the way his arms were folded across his chest. He stared at me sideways under the peak of his baseball cap. He didn't look impressed.

I was trying to think of something to say when suddenly his eyes darted away, he sniffed and looked directly at Josh.

"We don't want no Tina Turner," he said. "Tina Turner's yesterday." Then he walked away.

Josh followed him. "You can't cut her out just like that," he said. "Just because she did Tina Turner don't mean to say she can't do other stuff."

"She's too much, she wants to be a star. There ain't no stars in this band – just machines – we're techno."

"Yeah, but you said we had to be different . . . something to give us the edge; with her voice we'd be massive."

"If we need a voice we can sample one."

I waited and wilted, wiping the sweat from my forehead. I'd sung my heart out and now I was the subject of a full-scale argument. Nazim joined in, backing Josh.

"But she can perform live on stage," Nazim pointed out. "When people come to a gig, they want something to look at – not just machines."

Josh nodded in agreement. "We can be techno, rap, hip-hop, reggae, anything we like, but her voice – that's unique – know what I'm sayin'?" He put a hand on Tiger's shoulder. "Let's give her a try."

I held my breath whilst Tiger debated. He had to agree – he just had to. I watched him, willing him to say yes. Then with a sudden quick sideways movement he shrugged off Josh's hand and turned to face us. "OK. But if it don't work – she's out."

I breathed a long sigh of relief as he strode off. Thank my glittering stars, I hadn't totally blown it.

Josh came back to me. "Don't mind 'im, he just sore 'cos his woman left 'im. He'll come round."

I hoped so. "Can I get a drink?" I asked. I was hot and sweaty and needed a break.

In the entrance hall I guzzled a carton of orange juice gratefully whilst Josh leant his long back against the drinks machine, and looked down at me. He was wearing a yellow T-shirt and the same baggy khaki shorts he always wore, but somehow he managed to look good in them. He was so tall and lithe and elegant that he made any clothing look designer.

He was nodding his head and looking very certain about something.

"You're good, you know that, girl?"

"Yeah, I know that. But Tiger's not convinced. Maybe I'm not right for this band."

Josh laughed. "Tiger jus' fartin' with his mout', man. He don't know nuthin'. We ain't got no band yet. It just an idea. He's cool with all the techno stuff, but he ain't got direction. He jus' like playin' about with his software – surfin'. You know what I'm sayin'?"

"Sort of."

"Don't worry none. Jus' means he got too much money and not enough soul. His dad's in scrap."

"Oh, right," I said.

Josh laughed and clapped me on the shoulder. "He jus' a poor little rich boy, ya know. Come on, girl, let's make music."

We returned to the bare, dark hall where Nazim was practising drum rolls on stage.

"Right, we'll start from what we know and move on up," Josh said, picking up his guitar.

What we all knew took a few minutes to establish. Me with my gospel choir singing, Tina Turner and all the blues records Mum and Dad listened to; Josh brought up on Bob Marley and rap; and Nazim who liked bangra and anything with a beat.

We settled on Bob Marley's "Get Up, Stand Up". I knew most of the words and those I didn't, I made up. After half an hour we were knocking it into shape, Nazim doing some great drum fills and Josh impressive on guitar. I had to listen real hard and count when to come in. We were all concentrating so intently that we hadn't realized Tiger was back until he spoke from the doorway.

"Not bad," he said. "But we gotta make our own groove. Be original."

He strode forward, went over to his keyboard and did some complicated trills.

"You need to be in the studio to hear my best stuff," he said. "I'm workin' on this real atmospheric piece, begins with a great synthesized wash which gives way to a real driving drum beat and then I build it – layers of sound."

"How about you join in 'Get Up, Stand Up' for starters?" Josh asked.

I held my breath.

"OK, you're on," Tiger replied.

We played it several times. I was nervous, hoping I'd come in at the right places and aware that Tiger had said he didn't want my voice to dominate. I hoped I wasn't too loud but if I was going to sing then I would sing and I'd stand at the front and move around. That's what singers did.

On the final run through, my voice soared like it had been set free, and when we finished I was glowing, tingling with success. Something had clicked. It was as if I'd been plugged into the band, sensing where they wanted me to go. I looked out at the empty hall and had a sudden, blinding flash of hope – we could be good, we could be very good, we could be stupendous, mega, famous!

I looked over at Josh, and grinned.

He wiped the sweat off his forehead then gave me a thumbs up sign. "Man, we was jumpin'," he said.

But Tiger's face was grim. "We're fightin' each other. Goldie don't need to be so prominent, she should be just another instrument. And," he turned to Nazim, "we don't want no fancy drummin' – just keep the beat."

Nazim looked disappointed.

Josh sat down to tune his guitar. He plucked a few notes and said, "I'm not sure you're right. But we can try it your way. You game, Goldie?"

I nodded. I wanted to convince Tiger that I wasn't a prima donna, that I was willing to fit in and was ready to try anything. We played again and this time I kept my voice low and soft as Tiger let his keyboard soar. He seemed more satisfied, and when he suggested we meet on Wednesday night at his place we readily agreed.

"Come and see my studio. See where the real power of music lies," he challenged.

We packed the instruments away, then helped Nazim haul his drum kit back to Zoë's office where it could be locked up.

Outside there were women queuing for Sunday night bingo – a line of handbags and hopeful faces braced against the cool night air.

Tiger started off towards the far end of the square. "See ya Wednesday," he shouted over his shoulder.

I knew I was included and it made me feel like a real legitimate member of the band. I waved to him enthusiastically.

Nazim grinned. "You're in then," he said.

"I hope so."

"Course you are. See you Wednesday," he said, as he walked off towards the shop.

Left alone, Josh and I began to talk about the rehearsal but I was only half-concentrating. Over Josh's shoulder I could see some tough-looking lads staring at us. One of them was wearing a black, woolly hat pulled down tight and I caught the glint of an earring as his head turned. He was the biggest and bulkiest of the gang and I didn't like the way he was eyeing us up.

I interrupted Josh mid-sentence. "Josh, I've got to go, I. . ."

Too late. The big lad was coming towards us, heading a posse of his mates. Baggy jeans, big anoraks; they walked with that easy, loose-hipped stride as if their limbs had been greased. I saw Josh's shoulders tense; his eyes darted nervously from one to the other.

"Hey man," the big lad greeted him.

Josh slapped hands with him but sort of half-heartedly, I thought. Bull-necked and solid as a baseball bat, the lad looked at me. His stare went up and down and through me. His lip curled.

"You found yourself a woman, eh?" he said to Josh.

Josh put his hand on my shoulder. "This is Goldie. She's new here. I'm watchin' out for her."

The big lad's eyes flashed. He turned his headlamp stare on me. "Everythin' to your likin'?" he asked.

My tongue seemed to melt in my mouth, I couldn't answer. I just wanted him to go away but he kept on staring.

I noticed a small scar on his top lip, a thin stripe of hair running from earring to chin, framing his heavy jaw. He sniffed and spat, then spoke again.

"I ask you if everythin' all right?" he said, his tone gruffer now.

I looked away from him, mapping a line of escape, but he stepped closer. Although he wasn't much taller than me, I felt dwarfed by his bulk.

He cocked his head back and looked down at me. "You cool, baby?" he asked.

I nodded and tried to look cool though I really wanted to run.

"How old are you?" he asked.

His jaw seemed like a solid rock face above me, his neck was swollen with bulging veins.

"Fifteen," I answered.

He looked me up and down again. "You cool, all right," he said, and he laughed, showing a glinting gold tooth.

Abruptly the laughter subsided and his face set into tight, mean, lines. "You black?" he asked. "You call yourself a nigger, girl?"

His eyes fastened on me. I could feel their power pulsing towards me like thousand-watt lamps. My heart thumped loud as a bass drum, blood pumped in my ears. I knew what he was getting at.

I could feel Josh willing me to give the right answer but I couldn't betray my family. Long moments ticked by, no one spoke, there wasn't a sound. Finally I steeled myself and looked the brutish lad in the eye.

"Me – I'm no colour," I said, quietly.

His face tightened and he let out a harsh, rasping breath. "You think you livin' in the suburbs girl? You think you livin' in some nice middle-class community? Let me tell you somethin', we livin' in a war zone 'ere. You got to know whose side you on. You gotta choose. I'm givin' you an opportunity 'ere, girl, an' you better take it. Are you a sister? Are you black?"

I hesitated, felt Josh's hand tense on my shoulder.

"Yes," I replied. "I'm black."

CHAPTER SIX

Monday morning. I was awake at six-thirty, dry-mouthed and tense, my head still full of dreams. I padded to the bathroom, the cold floor making me shiver; my stomach twisted nervously as I sat on the toilet. I studied the black and white tiles making first the black and then the white leap up at me until my eyes were dazzled. Soon I'd meet Miranda at the school gates. Then, I'd be swallowed whole; channelled down a maze of corridors, poked, prodded and examined before being spat out at the end of the day.

I shuddered. A massive school full of people I didn't know – a foreign country full of swamps and booby traps. I started to feel sick but then I told myself I was being over dramatic. After all, I already knew three people: Miranda, Josh, Nazim. Three down – one thousand, two hundred and ninety-seven to go. And it wasn't as if I was new to the comprehensive jungle – I'd been there before, I'd worked out some survival rules.

I sat and contemplated:

Rule one: Don't draw attention to yourself.
Rule two: Don't offer any information about yourself unless asked. Remember anything can be taken as evidence and used against you later.

Rule three: Don't let anyone know you're clever.
Rule four: Pretend to hate what they hate and like what they like.
Rule five: Check out what everybody else is wearing and try to blend in.

Five good, sound rules. I should publish them. "The Beginner's Guide to Comprehensive Schooling". Whether I could stick to them was another matter. Anyway, time to move on, I'd been sitting on the loo so long that my bum was numb.

I decided I'd feel better if I washed my hair so I dug out my favourite papaya shampoo, stuck my head under the pitiful dribble of the shower attachment and tried to imagine that I was standing under a tropical waterfall. As the foam frothed over my shoulders and slid down my hips I sang my blues – calypso style:

"Gotta go to a new school,
Gotta obey some new rule,
Gotta get me an education,
But I mustn't draw no attention
Gotta act like I don't care
Even if the teachers, they despair
Gotta smile if I get detention
'Cos my friends say we cool, we gonna follow no rule,
'Cos we's no fool. . ."

I laughed at myself. My blues had turned to rap – crap rap. As I rinsed out the suds, I ran out of rhymes and someone was hammering on the door.

"You giving a concert in there?"

It was Dad.

"I'll be out in a minute."

"Good. I've got to get to work."

I wound a towel round my wet hair, then grabbed the biggest towel I could find, wrapped it round my body and wandered out.

Dad was standing on the landing in his boxer shorts.

"Sorry. Just making myself beautiful," I said.

"No wonder you took so long," he retorted, pushing past me.

I gave a loud "huh" and flicked my fingers at his retreating back. He yelled something inaudible and I fled into my room.

One of the great luxuries of having my own bedroom was being able to wander about half-dressed. I'm not the embarrassed type but when your body's changing, you need time to settle in with it. Finding privacy when sharing a room with Patrick had presented a big challenge. One morning I was dressing and thought Patrick was asleep, when I suddenly saw his eyes, big as gobstoppers, staring at me.

Later he took great delight in telling Mum, "Goldie's boobs are blowing up."

Mum told him it was rude to stare and later that week I walked in when she was giving him the lowdown on puberty. After that, I'd dressed behind the wardrobe door. But now, in my own room, I could dance, exercise, pose, lie down, pick my nose or do whatever the hell I wanted to – in private. The freedom was heady.

I gyrated over to the mirror. It was a big gilt affair that Mum had picked up from a junk store. There was a slight crack in one corner and it was mottled with black spots, but by dodging I could see well enough. Up close I could see all of my head and shoulders, and if I stood on my bed then I could view shoulders to thighs.

I peered closely, shaking out my long black hair, coiling it over one shoulder and pouting my lips. Yes, great publicity shots – S–E–X–Y.

"Goldie Moon – lead singer of top pop group 'Moon Dog' – says success has helped transform her life. She's recently moved from a desolate north London housing estate back to the area where she was born."

"I bought the family a lovely house with a huge garden and I love to go back there when I return from my world tours," said gorgeous, dark-eyed Goldie. "My roots are here, but I have also bought a house in Jamaica."

"And is there any truth in the rumour that you and lead guitarist Josh are engaged?"

"No, we're just good friends."

I struck my most superior pose and waved away the reporters. Then I caught sight of my reflection, and I grinned at myself. But maybe my fantasy wasn't so incredible. After only two days on the estate I was already in a band, and hopefully after Wednesday's practice, I'd be a permanent member. And who knows what would happen after that?

Every time I thought seriously of myself daring to sing at the Community Centre, I cringed with embarrassment. But a part of me felt excited and proud too. I'd really gone for it – sung as well as I could. OK, I felt a bit stupid when Tiger said Tina Turner was yesterday, but he hadn't actually turned me down and Josh and Nazim thought I was good. They weren't just saying it to be kind, I'd heard the enthusiasm in their voices.

More than anything, I wanted to sing; to be on stage with everybody listening and dancing. Gran used to say, "Goldie, you God's sunshine. You make people happy when you sing."

Well, I didn't know whether I believed in God any more. I sure went off him the night Gran died. But if I could sing, be famous and help people have a good time, then that's what I wanted. I pouted into the mirror once more and smiled my warmest, most alluring smile before turning to get dressed.

I didn't look quite so hot when I put on my school uniform. Maroon sweatshirt, grey skirt, maroon socks – most of it bought from the second-hand shop. I felt like a bottle of red wine. Funny word "maroon". Maroon, maroon, macaroon. The more I said it the dafter it seemed.

The good thing was that it suited my colouring. My skin shone a rich chestnut brown with no hint of yellow. The skirt was second-hand and a bit long and the shoes were way out of fashion. But I didn't look a total wreck. I was slim, despite all the fast-food takeaways I'd eaten when Gran was ill. I wished my nose wasn't quite so flat, but my eyes were big and dark. Dad always said my eyes were just like Mum's. And Mum had beautiful eyes.

I did a few dance steps and my supermodel pose, then went down to the kitchen where Dad was eating toast.

"You look smart," he commented.

I made a wry face and gave an exaggerated twirl. He smiled, his blue eyes gleaming softly.

"How you feeling about starting work?" I asked.

He licked his lips and swallowed. "Nervous," he said.

I went over and put my arm round him. Tendrils of damp hair clung to his forehead. Brushing them aside, I leant down and kissed him.

"You'll be fine," I said.

Patrick came clattering down, all excited about his new school, and looking important because he was wearing a uniform for the first time. He was dressed in maroon and grey too. His striped tie dangled unevenly – one long thin piece hanging down to his knees and the other fat end stuck under his chin like a bow-tie.

"I don't think my tie's right," he said.

"No kiddin'?"

"Help me do it," he pleaded.

I rinsed my buttery hands then thought better of it. A tie could take all morning. "Ask Dad," I said.

Mum swept in, all apologies. "Hey, what you doin' all gettin' up before me? I supposed to be the perfect mother today. David, why you let me lie in till this time?"

"Not my fault if you're a lazy good for nothing."

He caught hold of Mum, pulling her on to his knee and hugging her. She laughed and kissed him.

"My man's goin' to work today. He bringin' home the bacon," Mum said, as she got up and danced over to the kettle. And she began to sing Stevie Wonder's "Isn't She Lovely" but of course, it was "He" in Mum's version.

I retreated to my room, toast in hand. It was good to hear Mum laughing and singing, she certainly deserved to be happy – I just wished I felt as chirpy. I nibbled at my toast and eventually gave up and concentrated on trying to tame my hair. I oiled and combed it to stop it going wild, then scraped it back into a ponytail. I put my old school books into my bag, fitted a new cartridge to my pen and zipped my dinner money into my blazer pocket. At least I'd be able to pay for dinners now Dad was working again. I'd hated being on the freebie list.

Dad shouted up the stairs. "Goldie, I'm leaving."

I ran down to find everybody standing in the hallway; Dad looking smart enough to be the boss in dark grey jacket, black trousers, white shirt and striped tie. Mum had ironed everything so sharply that it all looked new.

"You look great, Dad," I said. "They'll promote you on sight."

"The job I've got will do for now," Dad said with a grin.

Mum beamed at him as she handed him a packed lunch and flask.

Dad kissed Mum and Patrick, then me. "Good luck at school," he said. "Hope it goes well."

"And the same to you," I said, smiling up at him. His hair had got a bit thinner recently and there were two deep lines running from his nose to the sides of his mouth, but he was still very attractive, his eyes blue as sapphires, his smile tender as moonlight. A lot of people thought he looked like Sting but I thought him more handsome.

We all watched him leave, lunch box under his arm, limping slightly but still managing to look elegant and graceful. Before he disappeared under the bridge, he turned and waved.

"Hope he gonna be all right," Mum whispered.

"Course he will be," I reassured her.

I gave her a quick hug, then ran upstairs to get my rucksack; I found an apple and a bag of crisps in the kitchen and said goodbye.

Walking through the estate, I hoped I'd see Josh but there was no sign of him. Groups of maroon kids clustered together, laughing and pushing each other towards the main road but there was nobody amongst them that I recognized. Feeling conspicuous, I dropped behind and kept to the shadows of the flats until I was out on the main road, where I lost myself amongst the crowds walking toward the school gates.

I thought I'd never spot Miranda but near the main drive most pupils disappeared up side-pathways and I saw her standing by herself. She was looking worried, her eyes scanning the pavements.

"Thought you weren't comin'," she said.

"Sorry, I didn't want to be too early."

"Well, you was nearly late. Hey, Joe," she shouted to a passing boy. "This is the new girl I was tellin' you about. Pretty, ain't she?"

A tall, lanky lad with greasy black hair came over and peered at me. "Yeah, not bad. Got a boyfriend?"

"No, an' she don't want one neiver," Miranda said. "Leastways, not you."

"What's wrong with me, then?"

"Nothin' the plague wouldn't cure," Miranda giggled.

She pulled my arm and turned me away from Joe.

"You don't want to have nothin' to do with 'im," she said. "Anyway, he's always after me." Still giggling, she pulled me towards the main drive. "Come on, I'll show you where the office is. They'll let me wait with you."

As we went up the drive Miranda shouted to several people. "This is Goldie, she's new. I'm showing her round."

I looked down at the ground. Rule number one: don't draw attention to yourself. I should have explained my rules to Miranda.

By the time we reached the office it seemed to me that half the school knew my name. Miranda was waving and advertising me like I was a new designer label. I was feeling over-exposed, trillions of eyes glaring at me with curiosity. I wished I'd had the sense to creep in quietly by myself. I wished I'd never relied on Miranda.

The bell went and all pupils disappeared, but we were left standing in the corridor waiting for a teacher to come and collect us. Next to us was the window where latecomers had to register, and I became aware of someone staring at me.

"Well, if it ain't the new kid on the block."

My head jerked back in surprise. It was the yobbo who'd asked me last night if I was black. I hardly recognized him without his hat. His head was shaved at the sides, the hair on top forming a hard square brush. But one thing about him hadn't changed, even in school uniform he looked threatening; his striped tie pushed to one side by bulging neck muscles and a maroon blazer gaping open to reveal his massive chest. When he came towards me, I prickled with fear.

"First day 'ere?" he asked.

I nodded.

"Keep ya 'ead down. Any trouble, see me, OK?" he instructed.

I nodded again. I couldn't meet his eyes but I watched as he walked back to the window and gave his name.

"Wes Mabbott."

Neither Miranda nor I spoke until he walked away, then

she said, "You don't lose much time, do ya? First Josh, now Wes. You're well in, ain't ya?"

I shrugged. "I just saw him last night after the band practice."

"What band?" Miranda's eyes were like gobstoppers.

"Oh, it's nothing," I said, cursing myself for having mentioned it. "I mean, I was messing around, singing a bit with Josh's band."

Miranda gulped like a fish needing air. "Oh, my gawd. Now you're in a band too. Fast worker, ain't ya? Still never mind. If Mabbott fancies you, you're made."

I looked down at the grey speckled floor. "He doesn't fancy me. At least, I hope not."

Miranda's hand moved down to tap me lightly on the arm. "Mabbott don't notice yer for nothin'. You'd do well to keep in wiv 'im. Everybody's frightened of 'im."

"I'm frightened of him," I replied.

I was privately thinking I didn't want friends like Wes Mabbott. I'd prefer to choose my own friends, friends that didn't look like they'd exterminate you if you disagreed with them. I was just wondering why every time I opened my mouth, stuff kept jumping out, when Miranda asked in a loud voice, "Are you a real good singer, then?"

A class was trooping past on their way to assembly and several pupils turned to look at me. I shuffled uncomfortably.

"Not really," I said quietly. "I told Josh about singing with the choir and he said why didn't I have a go with his band."

"Well, don't worry. I won't tell nobody," Miranda said.

Then she was silent as a tall, thin pale-faced woman with silvery blonde hair came towards us. Dressed all in black, she looked forbidding but her smile was bright.

"Hi. I'm Mrs Newman. You're Goldie?"

Her carefully made-up eyes looked at me questioningly, her pale eyebrows raised in two thin arches.

"Yes, I'm Goldie Moon," I said.

"You're in my form – 10N. I hope you'll be happy with us. They're not a bad lot. We get along pretty well. Miranda, you can go to your own class now, thank you. I'll look after Goldie." I turned and watched Miranda's retreating back – I was on my own.

CHAPTER SEVEN

The loud chattering ceased abruptly as Mrs Newman led me into the classroom. I stood nervously at the front whilst curious eyes inspected me.

Mrs Newman beckoned to a girl at the back of the room. "Charlene, could you look after Goldie today?" she asked.

A girl with pale lank hair and cheeks as big as moons lumbered towards me. She folded her arms and stared, her dimpled chin sagging on to her chest, pink-rimmed eyes sizing me up. I tried to smile encouragingly but my mouth froze. For a few tingling seconds I stared down at my shoes.

"She new?" I heard the girl ask.

Mrs Newman replied that I was and asked the girl if she would take me to first lesson when the bell went. There was an agonizing pause before Charlene agreed. A sense of relief washed over me; better to have this girl a friend than an enemy.

"I'll take care of yer," she said. "You can come and sit at our table." I followed her to the back of the room. She pulled a chair out for me, almost unseating another girl in the process.

"Don't worry," she said, when I'd sat down, "this school ain't so bad – not as bad as some."

I wondered how many schools she'd been to.

"Could be worse," she went on.

"Oh, yes," I said.

"I'll look after yer, show yer where to go."

There was something about Charlene that didn't encourage long conversations but she was thoughtful enough and guided me to my first class. In the corridors she made a useful shield, tackling the crowds like a prop-forward in a rugby scrum, leaving me to trail freely in her wake.

In English she sat beside me and showed me her predilection for drawing cartoons – the Spice Girls, Bart Simpson, Minnie Mouse – all executed with delicacy and skill. At break she hung around, minding me, while other girls asked lots of questions. This time, remembering my rules, I doled out minimal answers.

Lessons presented no difficulty, though I'd done much of the work before and was slightly bored. Lunch time was a problem. Charlene had a prior arrangement and left me in the care of others who wandered off expecting me to follow.

I was lost in a river of blazers and sweatshirts and lots of bobbing faces that I didn't recognize. I was beginning to panic, looking for a friendly face to guide me to the cafeteria, when miraculously I saw Josh. At first I wasn't sure it was him because he looked the same as everyone else, part of the maroon tide, but he was taller, and his long dreadlocks and loose elegant stride marked him out.

I tried to reach him but couldn't quite make it so I shouted his name. He turned, recognized me and beaming across the heads between us, shouted a greeting.

"Hey Goldie. How ya doin'?"

He pushed through to me, nodding and smiling, and placed a hand on my shoulder.

"Almost didn't recognize you. You look different."

Of course, he hadn't seen me in school uniform either.

"Different but the same," I said, indicating all the other kids.

"Yeah," he agreed.

He guided me towards an empty doorway.

"I'm glad to see you. I was lost," I said.

"You headin' for dinner?" he asked.

"Yeah. But the girls I was with have all disappeared."

"No sweat. Come with me."

Walking the corridors with Josh I felt comfortable and safe. Everybody seemed to know him. He slapped hands in greeting and a couple of people clapped him on the back and asked who I was.

"This is Goldie," Josh answered with a big grin but said nothing more.

We joined the queue outside the dining hall, standing quietly as kids jostled and shouted around us. A dinner lady with a furious red face was turning back kids who were trying to push to the front. I stood beside Josh, shielded from the fray.

"Feeding time at the zoo," he quipped.

I nodded, telling myself it would seem less threatening when I actually knew the kids who were elbowing me.

When we finally got inside, Josh grabbed a tray and I followed suit. There was lots of choice: salads, chips, burgers, pizza, but I couldn't see how much things cost. The dinner ladies didn't give you any time to choose either, before they were barking, "Move along" and "What do you want?" And behind me, people were impatiently rattling their trays. So, I played safe and chose exactly the same as Josh. I wasn't particularly fond of pizza but it would do for today.

Josh added apple crumble and custard to my tray. "You need sustenance in this place," he said.

We walked into the middle of the hall looking for a place to sit. Suddenly Josh stopped dead and my tray hit his back.

"What's he doin' in 'ere?" I heard him mutter.

I followed the direction of his gaze and saw Wes Mabbott sitting with another black lad. Josh swerved towards a different table but too late, Mabbott had seen us.

"Hey Josh, my man. You and your friend sit 'ere," he shouted.

I sensed Josh's reluctance but he could hardly pretend he hadn't heard. Wes made a sharp sideways gesture towards some younger lads and without a word they picked up their trays and went in search of a new table.

"Us brothers gotta stick together, hey?" Mabbott said. "Hey, Ralph?" he asked the lad next to him.

Ralph nodded, his bare scalp shining. "Get some dodgy characters in 'ere," he said.

Wes laughed – a loud sneering laugh and my mouth went dry. I hung back not wanting to sit down but Mabbott motioned me to join them.

"Come on, girl. Plenty a room," Mabbott said, indicating the empty chair across from him.

I sat next to Josh, placing my tray opposite Wes as quietly as I could, trying to make myself small and invisible. But it was no use, his stare was like an X-ray.

"How ya likin' this place?" he asked.

The way he spoke was creepy; the vowels sliding over his tongue like slime.

"It's OK," I replied.

Thankfully he didn't press me further but focused his attention on his dinner, shovelling in mashed potato, smacking his lips and belching loudly. I looked down at my pizza and suddenly didn't feel hungry. It was a surprise when I glanced at Josh to see him casually sipping orange juice and looking as relaxed as if he were in a bar.

"Not often I see you in 'ere," Josh said, looking across at Mabbott.

"Just checkin' it out. We got some business, ain't we Ralph?"

Ralph chuckled, tomato sauce oozing from the corners of his mouth. He swallowed a big mouthful of food, then grinned at Josh, his smile creasing the dark brown skin at the edges of his bare scalp. "Yeah, we got some business."

Mabbott lowered his fork and leant forward. "You 'eard anythin' about Wraggy's lot extractin' dinner money?"

Josh's eyes grew big and round. "No, I ain't 'eard nothin. But it wouldn't surprise me."

"Ralph reckons they're totallin' a hundred quid a week. I got some of ma men sussin' it out but you jus' keep them peepers open, Mister Jesus Jackson. If ya see it 'appenin', we want to know. If ya 'ear about it 'appenin, we want to know. Got it? You got that, bro?"

Mabbott prodded Josh's arm for emphasis, leaving a splodge of gravy on Josh's blazer. Josh made no move to wipe away the stain; it stayed where it was – a shimmering, brown, slimy blob.

My heart was thumping. I'd seen thugs like Mabbott before but I'd never been involved with them. I couldn't get rid of the feeling that I was in a film, one of those violent films about LA gangs or a documentary on Brooklyn. I think Wes Mabbott thought he was in one, too. He'd studied the language, the swagger, the attitude. Even the heavy-handed way he ate his food smacked of violence.

I winced as he suddenly pushed back his chair with a loud scraping noise and sent a bowl spinning down the table.

"This pudding's crap," he said loudly. "Call it chocolate, it's more like shit. It is shit. I ain't eatin' in 'ere no more. This place serve garbage."

I held my breath as I watched the bowl shunt to within a millimetre of the table's edge. Then, in the ensuing silence, I breathed out, making a sort of nervous snorting noise. Desperately, I put my hand over my mouth, but it was too late. The snort sounded like laughter and Wes heard me.

His eyes were like a snake's, fixing me with a beady stare. I tried to think of something funny to say, a witty comment that might break the tension and excuse my laughter but my sense of humour deserted me. I dared myself to look at him; to meet his eyes. Two dark glittering beads glared back at me; hard as stone. My stomach lurched.

He was gripping the back of the chair; the fingers of his big hands spread wide. I imagined him lifting the chair and axing me with it. Then I saw his hands relax, loose their grip and amazingly, he smiled.

"I bet you taste good, girl," he said. "Bet you taste better than this shit . . . yeah? Bet you taste reeeeal sweet."

His tongue flicked out and wiggled from side to side then slowly, he ran it round his lips, nodding his head repeatedly and smirking suggestively before he turned to go.

The dining hall was silent. I heard no sound. Everything around me seemed frozen into stillness. I gripped my knife until the handle imprinted itself on the palm of my hand and I felt blood pulsing through my wrists and arms.

I watched Wes Mabbott walk away, knowing I'd done something stupid. I hadn't wanted him to notice me, I'd wanted to be invisible. Fat chance.

Beside me Josh let out a long low whistle. Then he said quietly, "You riskin' it, Goldie."

I wanted to say I was sorry, that I hadn't meant to laugh at Wes but I was so miserable that the words sank down to my stomach. I stole a look at Josh's face; he was chewing, slowly, thoughtfully. I hoped he wasn't angry with me.

Pizza turned to cardboard in my mouth and I sat in silence as Josh ate his apple crumble. The blob of gravy on his sleeve was solidifying – I wanted to wipe it away.

I'd made my mind up to say something just as Josh started to speak but then we were both interrupted by a chirpy voice behind us asking, "Mind if I sit with you?"

Neither of us replied but Miranda sat down anyway and immediately started to talk.

"Saw muscle man Mabbott wiv yer. What's 'e want?"

I looked at Josh.

He ignored Miranda's question. "Do you want that apple crumble?" he asked me.

"No," I answered.

Josh polished it off in three scoops, wiped his mouth on the back of his hand and said he had to go. Miranda tried asking him again what Wes wanted.

"Wes, always up to somethin'," Josh said enigmatically. Then he turned to me. "Gotta go. Basketball practice. See you Wednesday if I don't see you before. Meet me about seven at the Centre, right?"

I nodded. "OK."

He pushed back his chair and stood up. Then I felt his hand brush my hair so quickly I wondered if it was intentional. I looked up.

"Take care," he said.

His eyes were gentle. I knew he'd meant to touch my hair and I knew I was forgiven. My heart heaved a sigh of relief.

"See you Wednesday," I said.

My eyes followed as he walked gracefully round the tables, carrying his tray like a practised waiter and striding out as if he had all the room in the world. I sighed.

"Nice, ain't 'e?" Miranda observed.

"Yes," I said.

She speared some chips and pushed them into her mouth. I waited whilst she chewed. Her cheeks were pink with excitement, I knew she was going to ask more questions.

She swallowed. "Likes you, don't he?"

"I hope so."

She smiled smugly. "Lot o' girls would like to go out wiv 'im but 'e's never interested. Not in anybody particular."

She was watching me carefully. I piled dirty plates on to my tray and wished I could escape but I didn't really have anywhere to go.

"So, what's Wednesday, then? Got a date?"

I hesitated. "Yes . . . no . . . I . . ."

"Well, 'ave yer or 'aven't yer?"

"It's band practice."

"Oh, right. I forgot . . . Miss Singin' Star – our very own Scary Spice. Can't keep pace wiv you, can I? In demand – Josh, Wes . . . *Top of the Pops*."

Her voice was sharp, her tone sarcastic.

"Well, you could come if you like," I said, recklessly.

"Where to?"

"Band rehearsal."

"What would I do? They wouldn't want me 'angin' around, would they?"

No, I was pretty sure they wouldn't – at least not Tiger – and I regretted the invitation as soon as I'd issued it.

"Well, perhaps not yet," I agreed. "But you could come and listen when we've got some stuff worked out. Give us your opinion."

Miranda's face brightened. "Like a critic, yeah?"

I nodded, then quickly changed the subject.

"Mrs Newman asked this girl, Charlene, to look after me. She looked a bit frightenin' at first but she was OK."

Miranda stopped chewing. "Charlene?" she asked.

I could see lumps of the sausage on her tongue.

I nodded. "Yes."

Miranda scowled. "You want to watch 'er."

"Why?"

"She's Andy Wragg's sister, you daft bat."

"Who's Andy. . .?"

"You know, Wraggy. Right 'ard case. All the white kids do as 'e says. 'Im an' Wes are always feudin'. You wanna keep clear of Charlene. She's a stirrer," Miranda said in a voice loaded with conviction.

"She seemed all right to me," I said.

Miranda grabbed my wrist and thrust her face close to mine. Her eyes bulged and her face puckered up in dislike. "Well she ain't. You don't understand 'ow things work round 'ere so you better take my word for it," she said sharply.

I didn't argue.

Miranda showed me where to stack the trays and dirty plates. As we threw our used cutlery in the deep washing-up bowl some lads knocked into us, pushing and shouting. Miranda grabbed hold of me and dragged me along after them. We were joined by others, all thronging towards the door and were carried outside. Then I heard the chant – "Fight, fight."

I hate violence but there's something about a crowd shouting and cheering; you just have to see what's going on. I peered over somebody's shoulder, then pushed to the front and saw two boys fighting. Well, to be more accurate, only one was fighting. A tall, muscular, black lad was pummelling a small scrawny white lad. Then the black lad stepped back, took a hard swing and knocked the smaller kid to the ground. There was a sickening thud as his head struck the concrete and blood spurted from his temple. He lay ashen and still on the floor, his head lolling to one side. I felt sick. I wanted to help him but I didn't have the courage to step in.

"Kick him, kick him," some of the crowd yelled.

The big thug stood, open-mouthed, panting, surveying the damage he'd done. When he saw the boy wasn't getting up, he smiled in triumph, spat on the ground then wiped his mouth on back of his hand.

The crowd were still yelling, egging him on to greater brutality but the victorious fighter turned away. He'd done his job. I heaved a sigh of relief that it was over and looked for Miranda. But then, in the corner of my eye I caught a sudden movement, so quick that I almost didn't see it, but I knew that one last kick had been aimed at the boy's head.

"Bully," I yelled.

A hand grabbed my shoulder and pulled me away.

"Wanna get yourself killed?" Miranda asked, a look of urgent terror on her face.

Then I saw three teachers running towards us. Some kids cheered as one of the teachers grabbed the tall lad with blood on his knuckles and marched him away. The other teachers knelt beside the boy on the ground, talking to him and inspecting his injuries.

"We'd better get an ambulance," one of them said.

I saw the other teacher was Mrs Newman. She straightened up and began to shoo the spectators away.

"Clear off. Just clear off," she shouted. "You're like vultures. Show's over. Go."

The crowd dispersed and I turned away, hoping the injured boy would be all right. Then I saw Mabbott. He was lolling against the dining-hall wall. He beckoned to me. I hesitated, looking around for Miranda, but she'd disappeared. There was no escape. Wes started walking towards me. My heart fluttered like a trapped bird. He was going to take his revenge on me for laughing at him, I knew it. But as he came closer, I saw he was looking pleased, triumphant – a smug, satisfied grin sat on his face.

"Not a pretty sight, eh?" he said.

I didn't answer.

"Things get a bit rough round 'ere sometimes. You gotta watch it, girl. Know what I'm sayin'?"

"I can take care of myself," I said.

He threw back his head and laughed, his gold tooth glinting.

Ralph appeared at his side. "Nice one, man," Wes said, clapping Ralph on the back.

Then he looked over at me. "I guess he got what he deserved," he said. "Can't have people demanding money, can we?" His eyes swept over me from head to toe. He smiled.

"Hey, you real cute, girl." He came and stood in front of me, licking his lips and nodding his head slightly. Then he leaned forward and spoke quietly. "You lightin' my fire – you know what I mean?"

I stared at him in disbelief. What trick was he pulling now?

His eyes glittered and narrowed and he gave a throaty gurgle. "Your family sure is a problem, though. See, them 'ouses is for white people, right? And us blacks, we have our own turf, right? We know where the enemy is then. Right?"

"Right," I said, slowly nodding my head.

It was as if I was hypnotized, agreeing with every stupid word. When he spoke again, his voice was soft and slippery – it made me want to throw up.

"Your dad's white, yeah? But you can't help that. You OK for a half-breed. You look black."

I stared at him in disbelief. Was this supposed to make me feel better?

He touched my cheek. I flinched.

"Somebody tol' me you Josh's woman – but you ain't, are you?"

I desperately wanted to say yes, but I wasn't and I didn't want to get Josh into trouble. I looked down and said nothing.

He bent so close that I felt his breath on my face. "You like 'im?" he asked.

I nodded.

"But you not his woman?"

I shook my head.

"You wanna be my woman?"

I shook my head again.

"You lost your tongue?"

I raised my eyes and looked right into his.

"I'm nobody's woman," I said, and walked away.

CHAPTER EIGHT

Mum was on a stepladder painting the sitting-room walls a lovely shade of deep yellow. Huge blotches of paint spattered her white shirt and dark hair.

"What do you think?" she asked, gesturing with her paintbrush to the bright new colour.

"Great," I replied.

"Not too yellow, is it?"

"It's very yellow, but I like it."

Mum grinned and filled in a bare patch with feathery strokes. Then she chuckled. "Thank the good Lord for that. Nancy took me to this place . . . quality paint at rock-bottom prices but you had to buy a job lot – all the same colour. Our bathroom be banana; kitchen – butter; bedrooms – marigold, sunshine, mellow yellow."

"Should be cheerful," I said.

Mum wobbled slightly as she reached higher.

"Careful, Mum."

"I'm OK. Jus' wobblin' as I work. Should I paint the ceiling too?"

"No, I'd leave it white."

She nodded. "How you get on at school today, golden child?"

"Fine," I replied.

But as Mum put down her brush, I turned away and walked into the kitchen.

"Just making myself something to eat," I shouted over my shoulder. I didn't want her to see my face.

I wasn't really hungry but if I hung around Mum would ask more questions and I didn't want to answer them. School had overwhelmed me, assaulted my senses and knocked me out cold. My brain was reeling and I could hardly function. I'd walked home in a daze.

Pulling a slice of brown bread from its polythene wrapper, I spread it with a thin layer of margarine, then dabbed Marmite round the edges. The dry, salty sandwich stuck to the roof of my mouth. I ran a glass of water and as I sipped the cold liquid I felt calmer and told myself that my day hadn't been all bad. Nothing dreadful had happened to me. Josh, Miranda and Charlene had been friendly and the teachers seemed reasonable.

But I couldn't rid myself of the dark shadows flitting through my head. Images of the fight haunted me – the chalky white face of the lad lying on the ground, the bright red blood smearing his forehead, dark clots forming in his blond hair. And again and again I heard the crowd chanting, "Kick him, kick him".

And I remembered Wes Mabbott watching from a distance; a smug sneery smile on his face. After the fight he'd beckoned to me, expecting me to run over like a well-trained puppy.

I banged my empty glass down on the worktop. All this racist stuff was mindless and I was furious with myself for not telling him so. My cheeks burnt when I thought of how weak I'd been – nodding my head and agreeing with his stupid ranting. *Black with black, white with white. So you know where the enemy is.* What a load of rubbish and I'd let him get away with it!

I slammed the Marmite jar back in the cupboard. You're a moral coward, Goldie Moon. You talk as much crap as Wes Mabbott. *Oh no, I don't think it matters about the colour of your skin, it's what's inside that really matters.*

Well, if that's what I truly believed, why didn't I have the guts to say it?

I swallowed the last bite of my sandwich and looked out of the window. I hated this estate; hated the soulless, moronic people that crawled all over it and lived in the dingy little cells. Oh, sweet Jesus, was I glad I'd met Josh. If it wasn't for him I'd have run straight back to Blackheath.

I ran myself another glass of water and, as I drank, Mum's voice coming from behind me made me jump.

"Drinkin' water? Why don't you make some tea, girl, and tell me about your day?"

She bustled over to the sink, paintbrushes in hand, running the taps until the sink was flooded with yellow.

"I can't fill the kettle while you're doing that," I protested.

"I can move. Bring it over 'ere," she invited.

But I wanted to get away. "I've . . . got some . . . homework to do," I said. "I'll go up to my room and talk to you and Dad later."

Mum watched as I edged towards the door. She was looking at me in that way she had, as if she were reading my skin.

"So, how was your day?" she asked again.

I had to disappear before I told her everything. It was unfair to burden her with all my worries when she was so cheerful and busy.

"Fine," I answered before zooming up to my room.

Once inside I closed the door and threw myself on the bed. My head was aching and I was breathing fast. I dug my feet into the eiderdown, tightening the muscles, then relaxing them: feet first, then legs, then thighs, working up my body. I closed my eyes but my head was full of swirling images as dark and menacing as a vampire cartoon. I looked up at the ceiling, focusing on the bare light bulb. Come on, Goldie, be positive . . . have a little faith, as Gran would say. Think of the good things . . . the band . . . Josh.

That did the trick. I felt a warm wash of pleasure flood through me as I pictured his face. I pulled my knees up, rolled on to my side and realized that the more I saw of Josh, the more I liked him. Apart from the fact that he was seriously gorgeous, he had a great sense of humour and was full of energy and ideas. And he seemed to like me. He'd been happy to take me to lunch and kind about showing me where to go and what I should eat. We were getting on fine till Mabbott ordered us to sit with him.

A knock on the front door broke into my thoughts. If that was who I hoped it was . . . I listened hard and heard Mum open the door, then ask whoever it was to come in. Quick as a shadow I tiptoed to the top of the stairs and peeped through the bannisters. But instead of dark dreadlocks, I saw Miranda's blonde head in the hallway.

". . . just visiting my Gran and I thought I'd call round. . ."

Mum's lovely musical voice floated up the stairs. "Goldie be glad to see you. I think she need cheerin' up. You'll find her in the front bedroom."

I dashed back to my room and sat on the bed. Miranda called my name and the door edged open. A sharp nose appeared, then searching blue eyes. When she spotted me she rushed over, her anorak crackling; boot heels snapping on the floor.

"Where did you get to after the fight? I saw you talking to Wes, then next minute you'd gone."

Her wide eyes brimmed with curiosity but I didn't want to tell her that I'd spent the rest of the lunch hour locked in a toilet cubicle, feeling sick.

"Oh, I had to go and see Mrs Newman about something," I said.

She stood in front of me, staring like she was boring holes in my head. Then she bent close and whispered, "What did Mabbott want?"

I looked away; her eagerness made me feel uncomfortable. And I didn't want to talk about Wes Mabbott.

"Oh, nothing much," I said, closing my eyes and lying back on the pillow.

For a few moments there was silence, then I heard Miranda sigh and the bed creak. When I opened my eyes she was sitting by my feet, arms folded, lips pouting sulkily.

"Well, you could show some interest," she moaned. "I was worried about you."

"Thanks," I said.

She squared her shoulders, puffed out her chest and smiled.

"Well, we're friends, ain't we?"

I nodded.

She kept on smiling, running her fingers through her short cropped hair, then she turned and grinned at me until gradually I realized that she had something important to tell me.

Coughing pointedly, she cleared her throat and said, "Ralph came to see me. He give me a message from Wes."

She said it slowly, pausing for dramatic effect and emphasizing each word like a newsreader. She looked at me expectantly and I knew she wanted me to ask what the message was.

"What did he say?" I asked, obligingly.

"Wes wants to see yer."

"Oh, does he?" I said.

Miranda leant forwards, her face lighting up with importance. "Yeah. Yer know what I fink, I fink he wants to go out wiv yer," she said triumphantly.

I sat up and decided I might as well tell her because she'd find out sooner or later anyway.

"He already asked me to go out with him," I said.

My voice was flat as a punctured tyre but that didn't stop Miranda reacting like an excited newshound. She shuddered as if a thousand volts had pulsed through her body; her bottom shot up in the air and she flung her arms wide.

"Oh, Goldie," she squeaked. "When? What did he say?"

"Some stupid stuff about me being his woman."

"And what did you say?"

"Told him I wasn't interested."

Miranda's silence said it all. We both knew I'd made a major mistake. But what was I supposed to do?

I got up and walked over to the window, looking out over the empty concrete space to the bridge beyond. The red splodge was still there, blotting out the words, but my mind still saw them.

Miranda came over and stood beside me. "Wes's not that bad, you know. When my Grandad had a heart attack, he phoned for a doctor then ran all the way from the square to tell Gran."

"Well, fine," I said. "So he's an athlete, but that doesn't make him a hero. I don't like him. I'm sure he was responsible for that kid getting his head kicked in. You should have seen him gloating."

"Goldie, Wes was nowhere near that fight," Miranda argued.

"No, but he controlled it."

Miranda picked up my abalone shell and examined it. "Funny, innit?" she said. "So brown and ugly on the outside but real beautiful inside."

"Just the opposite to Wes," I said.

She pressed her lips together and set the shell back on the sill. "He's not all bad inside," she said. "And if I was you, I wouldn't upset him."

I moved the shell to its correct position, next to Gran's photo, and sighed. Then I looked at Miranda. "I'm not stupid. I won't go out of my way to upset him. But I'm not going out with him."

Miranda shrugged and sat back on the bed. "Please yourself, I just came round to deliver the message."

"What exactly did Ralph say?"

"That Wes wants to see you tonight at seven in front of the Community Centre."

"Well I'm not going."

Miranda swung her feet to the floor and stood up with an impatient stamp. "Why should I care! It's your funeral."

"It might be, but at least I've made my own box," I said.

She stared blankly at me for a moment, scowled, then her whole face puckered. She must have been gathering a torrent of words to spit out at me because the next moment she released them.

"You think yer so clever, Goldie Moon. Just because you're in a band and Josh fancies yer. Well, I'll tell you somethin'. You don't understand nothin' about this place. I wouldn't 'ave even spoke to you if my Gran hadn't of asked me. So there. You wanna watch it. Folks round 'ere don't like people what's too big for their 'eads, an specially not if they're tar babies."

She paused for breath, glaring at me. Then, before she stamped out she said bitterly, "I tried to warn yer but you won't listen. Nobody crosses Wes Mabbott."

I stood staring after her as the door slammed. I could hardly believe what I'd heard. I was stunned. What had I done to deserve that? I hadn't figured on Miranda being my closest ally, my best buddy, but I'd thought we could be friends. Why was she so angry? It wasn't her that was in danger. It wasn't her Wes Mabbott fancied. Then revelation dawned – perhaps that was the trouble. Josh, Wes... she was jealous!

I flopped down on the bed and punched at the eiderdown. *Tar baby*. Where'd she got that expression from? All the years in Blackheath I'd never been called anything much, except pretty. I suppose I'd been protected – most people knew us; Gran had lived there for years, Mum all her life. One time, a new girl at school wouldn't sit next to me at dinner and the teacher made a big fuss, explaining how we were all made the same – like lollipops, same ingredients, different flavours. But I hadn't really cared, I'd just moved away and sat next to Chola.

Now, all of a sudden, my colour seemed a big issue. Damn this place. White gangs, black gangs. Why couldn't people just live together?

I slammed my hand down on the eiderdown, making dust fly up. It wasn't fair. Yesterday I'd been so excited – happy for the first time in months – Dad working, Mum smiling and me . . . in a band. Today, I felt as if I'd been pushed off the edge and was swinging in mid-air. And it was all because of stupid, bullying Wes Mabbott. But I wasn't going to let him rule my life. I'd hated moving here but now I'd got Josh for a friend and the band to look forward to. Life here could be bearable. Wes Mabbott was just one person, a schoolboy – he couldn't be that much of a threat, could he?

As I was changing out of my school uniform, I heard the front door open and Dad shout that he was home. Quickly I pulled on jeans and a T-shirt, smoothed my hair and ran down to meet him. He and Mum were sitting on the old sofa in the half-painted sitting room, their arms round each other.

"How was work, Dad?" I asked.

Dad laughed softly. "Well, I'm tired as hell. Reckon I'm out of the habit. But it was fine . . . good, in fact."

I went over to give him a kiss. "I'm glad," I said. Then I

fetched another cup and poured tea for us all. I asked lots of questions about the job, because I wanted to know, but also because it stopped Mum and Dad asking me about school.

Dad smiled and answered cheerfully. "Yes, I liked it fine... people seem OK. Job's so simple I'll have cracked it by the end of the week. Not quite what I'm used to but... it's a job. Could be chance for promotion later on."

When Patrick came back with tales of playing gladiators and scaling the heights of the playground climbing frame, our happy family was complete.

Later, when we all sat round Gran's old table, eating Mum's fragrant bean stew, I was the only one who had a problem clearing my plate.

Dad was in great form, teasing Patrick and making silly jokes about beans.

"What do you call an old bean? A has been."

"What do you call a bean in a marathon? A runner bean."

"What do cannibals eat? Human beans on toast."

"Please, shut up, Dad," Patrick begged.

But Dad was laughing and waving his spoon in the air.

"This is what I married your mother for – her delicious Cari... bean stew," he said, grinning.

Mum, sitting next to him, entered into the banter. She grabbed his hand and warned him, "You eatin' nothin' till you take that back. My cookin' indeed. I didn't cook nothin' till I married you. And you married me 'cos I was the most beautiful woman in Blackheath – wasn't nothin' to do with cookin'. You know that."

Dad laughed "OK, OK . . . it wasn't your cookin' . . . it was . . . your mother's cookin'."

Mum wafted her hand playfully across his face as if she was hitting him, then grabbed his hand and pinned it to the tablecloth.

"You lyin' through your teeth an' I hope they all rot and fall out," she said, fiercely.

"All right, all right, I surrender," Dad said, leaning over to give Mum a kiss.

Then he suddenly became all serious and put his hand on his heart and asked, "Did I tell you about the first time I ever saw your mother?"

I shook my head. I'd heard the story many times before but I loved to hear Dad tell it.

"It was one dark winter's night. A friend from university called me up and asked if I wanted to go to this dinner dance. I said, 'Not likely.' Wasn't my kind of thing at all. But he said, 'I've got four tickets, and if you don't come there's a gorgeous girl who'll be without a date.'"

"Was that Mum?" Patrick asked.

Dad smiled. "No, it wasn't. It was a blonde-haired girl called Suzanne . . . and very nice she was too."

Mum pretended to thump his shoulder.

Dad looked shamefaced, then continued. "Well, when we got there it was a posh do – white tablecloths, chandeliers, all the men in dinner jackets, bow-ties – and I was in my old cords. Suzanne went off to dance with a handsome chap in the right attire, never to return."

"And then what happened?" I asked, because this was the part I liked best.

Dad smiled. "So there I was sitting all by myself and suddenly the music stopped, the lights went up and there, walking across the room, was the most beautiful woman I'd ever seen in my life. So graceful and elegant – like an Eastern Princess. Skin smooth as chocolate, long red satin dress, hair piled high on her head like a crown and a smile that lit up the world. She sparkled. Made all the other girls look pale as milk. I decided there and then she was the one for me.

"Who was she?" Patrick asked.

Dad glowed with the memory. "Your mum, of course."

He took Mum's hand and held it. "Loved her from the moment I saw her. But it took me a while to convince her that she loved me."

Mum took his hand and they gazed at each other with such tenderness that for a moment we were all quiet, even Patrick – and I wondered if I'd ever find somebody who loved me as much as Dad loved Mum.

"And then you had Goldie," Patrick said.

Dad laughed. "Well, not just like that. It wasn't so simple. Your Gran had lined up a nice Jamaican doctor for her beautiful daughter. Cousin Henry. . ."

Mum was giggling. "That's not true, she never . . . and

anyway Mum loved you like her own son when she got to know you. She adored you."

The end of the sentence faded and she looked suddenly sad, haunted by memories.

Dad patted her hand. "Not everyone approved, though. Took time for some people to accept us. You find out who your true friends are," he said.

"Well, a body only need a few good friends," Mum said firmly. "And now we're 'ere and we makin' some more."

Dad nodded. "Yeah. Things are on the up again."

Mum kissed his cheek. "They certainly are," she said. "I'm considering getting me a job. Nancy came round today. Tol' me there's a position going at Patrick's school. Classroom assistant. Think I might apply."

Dad looked thoughtful. "I don't know, Yvette. With your qualifications . . . you should be teaching, not helping."

Mum pursed her lips. "I'd be quite happy not to have all that responsibility at present, thank you."

"OK. Fine," Dad said. "You want it. Go for it."

Mum nodded, then winked at Dad. "I can also keep an eye on my son while I'm there," she said.

Patrick made a face, but was soon smiling when Dad started cracking teacher jokes. I sat back, watching each of them in turn, Patrick, Mum, Dad. They looked happy and relaxed. If only I could feel the same way.

When we'd finished, I helped Mum with the dishes. She was humming happily as she swished soap suds around but my eyes were on the clock, warily watching the minutes tick away. I couldn't help thinking about Wes Mabbott waiting for me. I was so twitchy that I nearly dropped a plate, then I did drop a handful of cutlery. By the time the big hand touched seven I was so tense I could hardly breathe.

"Somethin' troublin' you, girl?" Mum asked.

I hesitated then made a decision. Putting the tea towel down I said, "I have to go somewhere . . . won't be long . . . OK?"

"No, it's not OK. I want to know where you're going."

I fished around for an excuse – the truth would take too long to tell and I had to hurry.

"Just got to tell Josh something. He'll be up at the Community Centre. Back by eight," I said breathlessly. And without waiting for an answer, I grabbed my jacket and hurried out.

As I skipped over the concrete, it felt good to be doing something positive. I had to sort this out. I had to tell Mabbott I wouldn't go out with him . . . not now, not ever.

As soon as I entered the square, I saw him. He was leaning against the Community Centre wall, smoking. As I approached, he gave me a cool, hard stare and blew smoke down his nostrils.

"I don't like being kept waiting by my woman. That's somethin' you're gonna 'ave to learn," he said. "You the one who waits for me, right?"

I shook my head. "Look," I said, in my bravest, most sincere manner. "I can't go out with you. My parents say I'm too young to have a boyfriend."

He frowned; his forehead developing deep creases and his nose wrinkling. He was wearing a black leather jacket and his hair was oiled, slick as a fish. I knew some girls would go for his hard, tough-guy image, but I thought he looked like a thug.

He took another drag of his cigarette. "Hey, I'll come and meet your parents. Show them you couldn't be in better hands – everybody round 'ere respect me."

He held out his hands, grinning. Then putting his cigarette in his mouth he reached for me. I dodged niftily to one side.

"I don't want to go out with you," I said firmly.

He stared at me.

"Why?"

I hesitated a moment then blurted it out. "I don't fancy you."

For a moment he looked as dazed as if I'd smashed an arm into his face, then, he clenched his fists and snarled. "Bitch. What you wanna say that for?"

Stepping back he looked me up and down.

"You don't know what's good for you, girl. You better learn who's side you on."

He looked murderous but I knew I had to keep calm and face him out.

"I'm sorry, Wes. But I can't go out with you," I said quietly.

His mouth pursed up and he hoiked and spat. "You wait, Miss Fancy Bitch with your tight ass and cute tits. We let it go that you was a half-ass nigger 'cos you said you was black. Well, wait till people come howlin' for your blood – I won't do nuthin' to stop 'em."

I saw the hatred in his eyes and knew I'd made a dangerous enemy. I saw his head go down, his fist rise, but I didn't move. I stared him out, my heart pumping, my throat dry. Then he shrugged.

"You's got a ugly nose," he said.

He turned, shouted to someone across the square, then gave me one last glare before he walked away.

I stood, blinking back tears of rage and fear. At least he hadn't hit me but I knew he'd come close. I knew I should escape, run home, but I was transfixed; standing, watching his retreating back. Although he was walking away from me he seemed to be growing bigger; shrugging off rejection, pulsating with anger, he squared his shoulders, his large shadow looming across the square. When he reached his mates he said something and they laughed – empty, jeering laughter that echoed round the buildings, rattling my teeth and shaking my body. I felt I was doomed.

And then, like a mirage, a skateboarder came round the corner, sailing into the middle of the square. Oh no. Not Josh. Not at this very moment. He was like a mouse running into a trap.

One of Mabbott's friends shouted, "Oh, look who's 'ere. The skateboard kid."

I felt tension flash like lightning, bouncing across the open space. I wanted to run to Josh and warn him but Mabbott was already there, standing in front of him.

"What you doin' 'ere? You better watch your step, Mister Jesus Jackson, Mister . . . nice guy Josh . . . u . . . a. You better choose your friends carefully or that board'll be down your throat and the wheels up your ass."

I saw Mabbott prod Josh with his fingers as he spoke. Josh could have skated away. I hoped that's what he'd do – get out of the square as fast as he could. But he got off his board and stood right in front of Wes.

"Hey man, what's wrong?"

I held my breath. I expected Mabbott to lunge at Josh and I felt so sick I couldn't swallow. But then Wes suddenly stepped back. "Ask your white bitch girlfriend over there."

Josh swung round, saw me and skated over. I felt suddenly cold, and shivered as I pulled my jacket closely round me.

Josh came to a halt in front of me. "Are you OK?"

I nodded.

"What you done to 'im now?" he asked, gently.

"He wanted me to go out with him."

Josh's face clouded. "And?" he asked.

"And, I said no, of course."

Josh let out a long low whistle and glanced in the gang's direction. "Girl, you in trouble. Nobody refuse Wes."

"Well they have now," I said, defiantly. I looked up at him from under lowered lashes. "What do you expect me to do? Go out with him just because everybody's afraid of him?"

Josh stepped off his skateboard and came closer.

"No, I don't. But we better watch out. Wes owes me some, so I can keep him sweet. Then we have to hope he lets it go. Finds other stuff to keep him occupied."

"Yeah, like beating little kids up."

"No, Wes don't get his hands dirty. He has his bully boys to do that job for him."

"I've noticed."

Josh shuffled nervously. "Look, 'anging round 'ere ain't gonna do us no good. Let's move."

He was right, and anyway, I wanted to go home.

"Come to my place?" I asked.

"Yeah sure," he answered, flipping up his board and catching it.

We walked into the lengthening shadows, between the blocks of flats where lights pricked the sky. We passed a group of kids, but there was no sign of Wes or his mates following us and, when we reached the wide courtyard, our spirits began to lighten.

Josh put me on his board and we scooted over the slab-stones. It hit a bump and I fell off and was laughing as Josh put his arms round my waist and lifted me back on to the board. Together we sailed home in the falling light. When we stopped at the gate, I felt Josh's breath warm on my neck.

"I'm glad you don't want to go out with Wes," he whispered.

I leant my head back against his chest.

"So am I," I breathed.

CHAPTER NINE

The evening of the band practice, Josh and I met in the square. We walked out of the estate, up the high street and turned into a leafy avenue. I was a bit overawed when we arrived at a tall, ivy-clad brick terrace with lots of windows and steps, leading up to a wide front door.

"Is this it?" I asked.

"Yeah. How the other half live, eh?" Josh answered, as we climbed the steps.

He rang the doorbell and the sound seemed to echo through lots of rooms. We heard footsteps and were splashed in light as Tiger opened the door. Just as we were about to go in, Nazim arrived, running up the steps behind us.

"Hi! Glad I caught you, thought I'd be late."

Tiger stood aside as we walked in, then ushered us up two flights of stairs to his studio on the top floor.

"Come in, come in," he said, motioning us into the small room, his pinched face transformed now by an excited glow.

I blinked in the glare of harsh spotlights, then stared in amazement at the massed equipment. Shiny black cubes were stacked on the floor and table, wires and cables snaking from box to box. In the centre a computer screen shimmered. Red and green lights glowed, switches and keys awaited transmission. It was a techno, modular, alien landscape.

Tiger, in tight black leather trousers, seated himself at the controls and surveyed his instruments – Commander of the Starship *Enterprise*. His shoulders were hunched, his body tense; he sat like a coiled spring, wired and generating energy which pulsed from the tips of his splayed fingers.

"Taken me a while to build it. See – there's me Apple Mac, 'ere's me mother board. Listen. I jus' done this great sax part."

I was taken by surprise as a vibrant, sobbing sax wrenched at the stuffy air. I imagined a golden instrument lurking behind the speakers, nimble fingers running over the keys, notes buzzing through the wires, brain cells spinning inside the boxes. But how to connect the music I was hearing with this spaceship? Music to me was life and soul – not modules.

"See, you don't need instruments, just keys and boxes. Look I'm running Cubase on the Apple that connects with the Morpheus and the Juno, and its all time-coded so I can sync-up with live vocals or guitars or whatever."

Tiger leant back and looked at us. "Great, innit?"

Awed and silent, we nodded our heads. We were like innocent novices, wide-eyed and worshipful.

Tiger was enjoying himself. "Listen," he said. "Sounds like the real thing. Strings, brass, guitars. . ."

We listened while rippling strings, vibrating woodwind

and mellow horns melted through the wires and out through the speakers.

"Spooky, innit? A whole ruddy orchestra in there. Now I'll play you some of me tunes."

He jumped up, jammed the door shut, then resumed his seat and motioned for us to sit down. We made ourselves some room on the cramped floor, Nazim in a corner, leaning against a steel table, Josh and I sitting together, knees bent, backs against the door, feet touching.

A jumping rhythm filled the little room, layers of sound and disembodied voices. Some of the tracks were simple and funky, with catchy refrains, while others had sophisticated arrangements with strings and brass. Tiger was talented and skilled, no doubting that.

When the music finished there was a massive, empty silence. No one knew what to say, we were knocked out; we hadn't expected anything so accomplished.

It was Nazim who spoke first, voicing what we all felt.

"Wow, that's brilliant, man. Blastin' tunes; you got a whole album ready." Then he coughed, cleared his throat and asked the million-dollar question. "So, er, why do you want us? You got everything, man. All the sound you need."

Tiger flexed his fingers and grinned. "Performance. All this gear's great, but it ain't much to look at on stage. I figure you got to have personality too."

"And that's where we come in?" Josh asked.

"Yeah. You play what I create."

"And we don't have no say in this? I mean, I got my own songs, too, you know," Josh protested.

Tiger looked at him. "You write songs, yeah?"

Josh nodded. "Yeah."

"Well, what I'm talking about is sound. Complete sound. Listen, you ain't 'eard nuffin' yet."

I stretched my legs – moving to a more comfortable position. I figured this was going to be a long session.

Tiger lunged at switches and cued into his keyboard. "Right . . . let's go."

An unearthly wailing jarred and jangled at my nerves. It stretched around the room, pushing back the walls until we were in a vast, echoing cathedral. A haunting clarinet played. Pattering voices snatched at the air, rising and becoming shrill, then shattering into a thousand pieces. The chanting rose again, becoming sharp and frenzied until it was like gunshot, fired into the air. Guitars swung high and bent behind the voices, then descended into a booming bass. A rhythm beat strong in an African night; flickering firelight, crackling logs, dark shadows and fear.

I was transported, the music making pictures in my mind. I stayed with it until the speakers were buzzing and booming with a strong pounding beat, throbbing dance music.

"Jungle," Tiger yelled, rocking in his seat.

I kept time, slapping my knees, tapping my feet. I was mesmerized, lost in the rhythms and only came to when it faded away and I heard Tiger laughing.

"Mind blowin', innit, eh?" he asked.

I was silent, nodding my head in agreement. My ears were ringing and I hadn't quite come down yet.

Josh was congratulating him. "It's brilliant, Tiger. Brilliant."

Tiger was beaming from ear to ear. "It is, innit?"

Josh spoke again, more hesitantly. "Yeah, it is . . . it is brilliant but. . ."

"But what?"

"Well . . . you can't sing it, can you?"

Tiger's grin froze into a tight grimace. He sucked in air then expelled it with a sharp hissing sound. "You don't need to sing it. It ain't 'Roll With It' – it's techno."

Nazim squirmed out from under the table and sat on his haunches, his face wrinkled with concern.

"Yeah, Josh realizes that and, like he said, it's brilliant. I mean I love it. But what he's saying is, guitar bands are making a comeback. People like singing lyrics and we've gotta go with the flow. Give the people what they want."

Tiger ignored Nazim's reasoning. He wanted his own show. And if he couldn't have it, he was content to sit there, hatchet-faced, his silence thundering his anger.

Tension crackled round the room. Nazim sat down again, Josh drummed his fingers on his knees. I saw Tiger square his shoulders and I was afraid he was going to explode and throw us out. We had to sort this, because if we didn't there wouldn't be a band, and I couldn't bear that. I wanted the chance to sing and I had to save that chance before it disappeared. Desperately, I tried to think of something soothing to say but Josh got in first.

"It's not that I don't like it, it's just that I'm wonderin' how we gonna do all that stuff on stage. I mean, it must take hours to set up."

"Course it does." Tiger rapped the side of the computer screen. "You have to be a genius to understand this stuff."

"Absolutely," I said.

"You what?" Tiger asked.

"Erm . . . absolutely," I repeated feebly.

Tiger stared at me with raised eyebrows, shrinking me to a microdot.

"Well, sassy Miss Tina Turner has pronounced," he jeered.

His sarcasm rattled me but I wasn't going to be made to feel stupid. I stared back.

"Actually, I liked it," I said. "And I've got an idea. If you could run that middle part with the low rhythmic chants, I might be able to sing something over the top. A sort of haunting bluesy sound with all those intricate rhythms underneath might work."

"Yeah," Josh nodded. "It could be brilliant."

Tiger looked at me doubtfully, then shrugged. "Right, you're on."

He touched some notes on his keyboard and I stood up and sang the words of an old spiritual, slow and sultry against the pounding beat.

I knew I was taking a risk and wasn't at all sure it would work. By the time I'd finished, nerves and heat were getting to me. I stood trembling, wiping sweat from my brow.

"Hey, that was wicked," Josh said.

Then there was silence – we were all waiting for Tiger's reaction.

He nodded his head, looking thoughtful. Then he sat back, folded his arms behind his head and said, "Yeah, it worked. In fact," he looked up at me and grinned, "it was bloody sensational. As far as I'm concerned . . . you're in."

I clapped my hands and gave a loud, ecstatic whoop.

The tension in the room dissolved, as we slapped hands with each other and Tiger, in generous mood, offered to get us some drinks. When he'd gone, Josh and Nazim collapsed on to the floor looking relieved, and I plonked myself down next to Josh.

"I can't believe it," I said. "He actually liked what I did. He said I could be in the band. Did you hear him? Isn't it brilliant? I'll practise all the songs real hard and I know I won't be singin' up front all the time. I mean, I know, sometimes, I'll just be backing vocals and I'm prepared. . ."

Josh put a hand on my arm, "Goldie, it's fine," he said.

I laughed. I'd heard myself prattling on but just couldn't stop. "Sorry, it's just that I'm real excited and I didn't think that Tiger would. . ."

Josh gave my arm a gentle squeeze and put his face close to mine. I saw tiny curls peeping from under his dreadlocks, long black eyelashes curling round luminous brown eyes and a line of fuzzy little hairs along his perfectly shaped top lip. My stomach went into squishy spasms as he said softly, "You're our singer, Goldie. Me and Naz, we always knew you was good. It was just Tiger that needed convincing, OK?"

I nodded. He withdrew his hand from my arm and I wished he hadn't. I wanted to lean closer to him, accidentally brush against him, feel his warmth. Bending my knees, I shifted sideways. If I moved my shoulder just a few centimetres it would rest against Josh's. But there was no time for romantic thoughts; Nazim was thinking of practicalities.

"What we gonna call ourselves?" he asked.

"I dunno," Josh answered, turning towards him so that sadly, there was more space between us. "People just goin' for one name at the moment. You got Oasis, Coldplay, Travis Prodigy – short and sharp."

"We could be different," Nazim suggested.

"How?" Josh asked.

"I dunno . . . well like . . . er . . . Queensmead Community Centre Youth Band Incorporated."

Josh shook his head. "That's inspired, man."

Nazim grinned. "OK, so I'm not the creative element of the band. Drummers are not known for their intellect. We just keep the beat, man, we primitive."

Josh laughed and clasped his hands together, "Amen, brother," he said fervently. "But ya know, I spend time thinkin' 'bout this las' night and I couldn't come up with a good name either. Wired or Shocked was about the best I dreamt up."

There was silence for a moment while we all tried to think of a good name. I raided my brain and came up with Smashed.

"Sounds like a load of druggies," was Nazim's response.

"Or potatoes," Josh added.

"Well you try then," I protested.

"What about Roots?" Josh suggested.

"Not bad," I said.

Nazim's face was a picture of confusion. "I can't think of nothin'," he said, as he scratched his head. Then he smiled. "But what I did think of is . . . we gotta have an image. Identity. All successful bands have a definite image."

"I think we should go for a multicultural thing," I said. "You know, a real colourful ethnic look. Nazim in Indian stuff and me in a tight stripy tiger dress."

Josh's eyebrows shot up. I hoped he was thinking about how good I'd look in that dress but he just said, "Nazim's people are from Pakistan."

"Oh," I said.

When Tiger returned and handed round drinks, Josh raised his can of Coke and, in his boldest Caribbean accent, proposed a toast. "'Ere's to us. We on our way, brothers."

We clashed cans and drank to our success, then Josh spoke again.

"We been thinkin' while you was getting the drinks, thinkin' 'bout band names. We gotta choose a good name for ourselves."

Tiger had a ready response. Chin jutting forward, he looked at each of us in turn. "No prob," he said. "I got that sussed. We're Tiger's Band."

Josh, Nazim and I exchanged glances; understanding flashing between us. We knew we could argue this out but it would take time, energy and create more friction. My eyes darted round the room desperately trying to think of another name. I knew diplomacy was called for. It was important that Tiger think he was in control but important for us to think we hadn't given in completely. I looked around at the stack of sound equipment, the tall black amplifier and had a sudden thought.

"How about No Fear?" I asked.

My suggestion was met with a wall of silence.

I pretended to be upset. "OK. Whenever you suggest a name for a band it sounds crap the moment you've said it. But No Fear's as good a name as any . . . and at least it *means* something."

I gazed imploringly at Josh and Nazim. This was an argument we didn't need.

Josh sucked in his cheeks, thinking for a moment, then he shrugged and nodded. "All right. It ain't so bad."

And big relief, Tiger agreed with him. "OK. Just for now," he said grudgingly.

Nazim added his approval and we clashed our cans of drink again. "To the new band, No Fear."

I felt a dig in my side. Josh was looking at me, a mischievous smile on his face. "Can't wait till we get our costumes," he whispered.

My heart thumped into a jungle beat and I felt the blood rush to my cheeks, but thankfully the others didn't notice because Josh was standing in front of me saying something to them.

"OK," he said. "So, No Fear, I want to play you some of my stuff."

We made space for him as he plugged in his guitar and away he went. I loved the way he played, his guitar slung down low, his head bowed, his eyes half-closed; his fingers rippling over the strings, making it look easy. He must have practised for hours . . . years . . . and I'd thought he was just a skateboarder! It had been a surprise the other night when I'd heard him play, but now he really showed what he could do. Intricate blues licks and hot rockin' riffs.

I could see Tiger listening intently, letting nothing slip by him. I hoped he'd like Josh's music, hoped it wouldn't be too traditional for him. But Tiger was in a mellow mood, now we'd all been suitably impressed by his electronic wizardry, and when Josh had played himself out, Tiger was magnanimous.

"Yeah, great. Reekin' with possibilities, mate," he said, slapping Josh on the shoulder. Praise indeed from Tiger.

We worked on one of Tiger's tunes, with Josh playing guitar and Nazim programming the drum machine. Slowly it began to take shape. I was fascinated watching the song grow; notes, chords, bars, keys, adding instrumentation and sampled voices. Josh and Tiger were doing most of the work, but I wasn't bored, I was completely absorbed in the process and when I got to add some vocals, it went well.

By the time Nazim left to help his Dad close up the family shop, we had a rough cut of the song recorded. We were all on a high, and I felt it was a good time to break. I still had homework to finish – even potential rock stars have to hand in English essays.

"I've got to go too," I said. "Thanks, Tiger, it's been fantastic."

Tiger actually smiled at me and was about to say something when Josh jumped up and grabbed my arm. "I'll walk home with you," he said.

I beamed at him, stupid with happiness. But of course, Tiger had to spoil it.

"Hey, watch it you two. Don't want you getting tooooo close. Lots of bands bust up because of broken love affairs."

A smug, knowing smile creased his face and I could quite happily have punched him. Josh obviously felt the same because he glared at Tiger before hurrying off downstairs. I followed and caught up with him on the first landing.

"I could wrap my guitar round his thick head," he muttered.

"Wouldn't waste good wood," I said.

Josh frowned and pursed his lips – Tiger had really rattled him.

"Ain't none of his business," he said, as he hurried down the next flight of stairs.

"No, it ain't," I agreed.

By the time we were down in the hall, however, Josh had recovered and was his usual cheerful self again, smiling to greet Tiger's mum.

"Have you finished?" she asked.

"Yes thanks, Mrs Barnes," Josh answered.

She fiddled with the zip on her designer top. Rings flashed on every finger; her long nails were perfectly manicured.

"I hope he won't be up there half the night again. We get complaints from next door."

Josh gave her a sympathetic look. "Well we done some 'ard work up there, he shouldn't be long, he jus' puttin' on the finishin' touches."

"Oh, good."

She looked relieved. Her hand moved from the zip to smoothe her brittle blonde hair. Josh moved towards the door. "We gotta go. Goldie's gotta get home."

I stepped round Mrs Barnes, catching a whiff of expensive perfume, the sort I'd only smelt on magazine flaps.

She smiled at me. "Hope you were all right up there – they treating you OK?"

"Fine," I said. "It was a great night."

"Treatin' her right? She be bossin' us about soon," Josh said, laughing as he opened the door.

Mrs Barnes leapt forward, half-closing the door as if she didn't want us to go.

"How's your dad, Josh?" she asked.

"He's fine, thank you, Mrs Barnes."

"I wish he'd call. Please tell him he's welcome to visit . . . anytime."

"I'll tell him, but he's real busy at work at the moment."

She looked disappointed. "Well, give him my best and remind him I'm here," she said, weakly.

We said our thanks and stepped out, down the broad stone steps, into the night.

"Tiger's lucky to have such a nice big house," I said, as the door closed softly behind us.

"Yeah, they're loaded but . . . it don't make 'em 'appy."

"She seemed very keen for your dad to go round."

"She lonely. Paul – Mr Barnes – he's always out, wheelin' and dealin'. She likes Dad, knew him way back. She look after me when Mum died."

"Oh, I see."

Josh had never really mentioned his mum; perhaps it was too painful. I glanced at him, trying to gauge the expression on his face, but it was in shadow. We walked on in silence for a few moments until I'd convinced myself that he was waiting for me to ask more. I took a deep breath.

"Do you miss your mum?"

Josh didn't seem fazed but answered right away in a clear even voice.

"Yeah, I do. Everyone say she was a beautiful woman. I wish I had time to get to know her better. Sometimes I get angry that she die and it bugs me that . . . that I can't remember her real enough."

We walked down the avenue without speaking and I felt Josh's sadness like it was my own. Josh's stride lengthened and I scurried to keep up. We turned into the main road, awash with shop and car lights. When we'd crossed the road, Josh spoke again.

"I try to remember what she look like but as soon as I get a picture, it fades. I remember her sitting on my bed reading me stories. I think I remember her voice and the way she laughed but, I dunno, it like water runnin' through my 'ands."

"I'm sorry," I said, reaching out and touching his arm.

Josh stopped and turned to face me, leaning close. For a precious, heart-beating moment I thought he was going to kiss me. I lifted my face but he just smiled down at me.

"Well, ain't no use beatin' my brain over it," he said. "She's gone." Then, turning away, he carried on walking and changed the subject.

"Tiger really gets off on all that electronic stuff, don't he?" he asked, as we turned into the estate.

"Yes," I said.

"It was brilliant, wasn't it? When we all played together it really gelled. Amazing how good we sounded. Brilliant. And, he likes you."

"Do you reckon?"

"Course he does."

"I'm glad," I said.

"Yeah, so am I . . . so am I."

The words hung in the cool night air, making my insides fizz so much, I thought I'd explode before I reached home. It wasn't so much what he'd said, but how he said it. Soft and sweet. I skipped along beside him, the words tasting like melting sugar on my tongue.

All too soon we were home. Josh held the gate open and I brushed past him, hoping he would stop me and take my hand. But he didn't.

"See ya around," he said, closing the gate.

"Yeah," I answered, "See you around."

Mum came into the hallway as soon as she heard me open the door.

"How did it go?" she asked.

"Brilliant. I'm definitely in the band," I said.

"Wow," she whooped, grabbing me and giving me a hug. "That's my girl. You deserve it and you enjoy it, you hear?" Then she released me and, typical Mum, added, "But it's late. Don't you be neglectin' your school work none."

I smiled and gave her a kiss. "I won't, Mum. I came back 'cos I had homework to finish."

"Good girl," she responded, patting my back. "But, don't be too long. It's nearly ten o'clock, now. Do you want me to bring you a drink?"

"No thanks, I'm fine. I'd better get going," I said, retreating upstairs.

In my bedroom, I immediately crossed to the window and looked out, hoping I might catch a glimpse of Josh as he hurried away. But all I saw was the empty concrete square.

Disappointed, I pulled off my shoes and sat down on the bed. But it was hard to keep still. My body felt so alive, my blood throbbing to a strong beat, every nerve dancing.

I breathed deeply and tried to calm myself. It was no use. Pictures of Josh kept invading my mind: snapshots of his eyes, his smile; the passionate way he played his guitar; his long legs bent up underneath him as he listened to the music; his warm shoulder next to mine. I wished he'd kissed me goodnight.

I got up, put on the light and went over to the mirror. I studied my face, then pursed my lips into a delicious kissable pout. Oh, yeah, baby, you . . . a star! I stepped back so that I could see nearly all of myself in the mirror. Tall, slim but shapely, smooth brown skin, pearly white teeth, gleaming dark eyes, cascading black hair – I was attractive, wasn't I? Even if my nose was a bit flat and my chin a bit too pointed. Josh did fancy me, didn't he? I hoped so. I really did.

CHAPTER TEN

I came out of the Community Centre on a high. We'd just had a great band rehearsal, finishing with one of Josh's numbers. I loved his songs; the tunes were simple but memorable and the lyrics raw and punchy. "You got to tell it like it is," Josh would say, and I tried to do him justice, singing with honesty and passion. Today Josh had joined in the chorus and I was ecstatic because our voices blended beautifully.

"You were great," Josh said, as we left the Centre.

"It's a good song," I replied.

A group of kids had gathered in the entrance.

"Hey, look . . . fans," Josh said.

I laughed, but a girl in a denim jacket pushed forward.

"Was that you singin'?" she demanded.

"Yes," I nodded.

"You're bleedin' brilliant, you," she said. "Can I have yer autograph?"

"I, er . . . I haven't got a pen," I said, blushing.

Beside me, Josh was giggling fit to burst. "Told you," he said. "You'll 'ave to get used to it." Then he walked off, jiving over to an empty bench opposite the Centre.

I followed and so did some of the kids and we watched as

Josh climbed up on to the seat and faced us. Spreading his arms wide, he grinned.

"Welcome to Wembley Arena. Put your hands together for the new, the great, the brilliant, the massive – No Fear."

"Is that the name of your band?" one of the kids asked.

"Yeah, man," Josh answered.

"It's crap," the kid said.

Josh laughed.

"I love, I love, I love, I love, I love No Fear," he sang. The kids giggled too and two old women who were standing a little way off turned to stare.

"Josh, come down, they'll think you're nuts," I said.

But Josh was into it now. He sang louder, playing snappy riffs on air guitar. He finished off with a big flourish and jumped down, landing at my feet. Some kids clapped and Josh bowed.

"You're mad," I told him.

He dodged in front of me and started shadow boxing, shouting, "We'll knock 'em dead, baby."

One of the watching women shouted, "That's right, love."

"What is it with you?" I demanded. "Why do all the old women adore you?"

In answer, Josh pouted his lips, wiggled his hips and gave a smug smile. "'Cos I'm so sexy, baby."

Of course, the kids who were still hanging around thought this was hilarious, but I pretended anger. "Baby? I ain't your baby, don't baby me," I said, putting my hands on my hips and talking in a stern, don't mess with me voice. Then, wagging my finger, I said, "You know what my gran say?"

Josh shook his head. "No, baby, what your gran say?"

"She say . . . she say . . . she say . . . I can't remember what she say . . . but I know, she'd say, 'Go for it'," I answered, starting to giggle.

Josh chuckled. "Oh yeah, I know, that old Caribbean saying – go for it."

And he continued laughing as he put his hand on my shoulder and levered himself high into the air, twisting round and landing in front of me.

Behind him I saw lads on bikes pedalling towards us. When they came within a few metres, they stopped and stared and I recognized them as the pests who'd buzzed us on the day we moved in.

"I think we'd better cool it, Josh," I said. "Everybody's watching."

He grinned and spread his arms wide. "Good – fame I can handle," he said. And just to show he didn't care a damn, he danced a few steps and began to rap.

"Them A & R men come knockin' on our door,
Wantin' to 'ear what the crowd shoutin' for,
This new band they call No Fear,
Their music somethin' you wanna hear,
The people shoutin' for more and more,
Fear gotta write songs by the score,
They get to number one and taste success,

Well, baby . . . you know the rest,
They ridin' about in limousines and. . ."
"*. . .the girl singer she look like a queen,*" I finished off as Josh hesitated.

He laughed and slapped my hand in a high five. "Hey, girl, you cool," he said, giving me a big hug.

My heart danced whenever Josh touched me so I didn't care that the boys were whistling and making stupid comments, but I was puzzled when I saw Josh suddenly tense and look alarmed.

"What's the matter?" I asked.

He didn't answer but grabbed my hand and pulled me across the square.

"What . . . what is it?" I urged.

"Didn't you see 'im?"

"Who?"

"Andy Wragg."

"So?"

"So, I like to keep out of 'is way."

"Why?"

"On account of 'e might kick my 'ead in."

"What for?"

"No reason."

"Then why?"

Josh led me round the back of the shops, skirting round crates and boxes. When we were out of sight he paused to catch his breath.

"Wraggy don't need no excuse. He 'ates me 'cos I'm black. Fancies 'imself as a big shot in the National Front. Goes round painting slogans – Blacks Out, Wogs Go Home – all that sort of crap." He squeezed my hand. "Best to avoid 'im if you can. Come on, let's cut across 'ere."

We crossed the service road behind Nazim's shop and picked our way over the scrubby grass. The ground was littered with tin cans, bottles and rusting scaffolding poles, but what Josh had said made me so nervous I didn't care what I trod on. My palm was sweaty as I gripped Josh's hand. I didn't want to bump into Andy Wragg, either.

He let go when we came to a big puddle and I jumped sideways, skirting round the water in the opposite direction. When I joined him, he'd stopped dead and was staring down at the ground. His foot was raised and he was rolling something underneath it and frowning deeply. Then he kicked out, booting the object on to a patch of gravel. It was a plastic syringe.

"Man, I hate this place," he said. He strode forward and smashed the plastic tube into the ground. "Sometimes all I see is filth and hate. Look at this shit!"

I looked down and saw another syringe half-hidden in the grass, and then I noticed rubber bands, sliced polythene bottles and rusted spoons.

"People hate each other and hate themselves," Josh said, as he kicked at the debris, scattering shining needles and cloudy plastic. "There ain't no respect," he snapped, abruptly stuffing his hands in his pockets and striding off.

I ran after him, skirting round thistles and jumping potholes until I caught up with him at a low wooden rail that divided the wasteground from the path. He slumped down on the rail and stared into the distance, his long legs bent underneath him. When he spoke he looked straight ahead as if he wasn't really talking to me.

"Too many people round 'ere messed up . . . 'cos of dope," he said, his voice full of bitterness.

His eyes narrowed and when he looked up at me his face was hard as stone, as if he were accusing me of something.

"My mum still be alive if it wasn't for this shit."

I gasped. "Your mum was a drug addict?"

"No. She collapsed, an' the man who found her was too stoned to get help."

His face was dark with pain. He rubbed at his nose, blinked and looked down, dreadlocks falling over his eyes.

"She had asthma . . . could 'ave saved her if they'd got her to hospital in time."

"Oh, Josh."

I wanted to reach out and comfort him, put my arms round him, but he felt too remote, too stiff and angry. He sat there breathing quick and heavy in the fading light and I couldn't help him.

"It a waste, man . . . a massive waste," he muttered.

Suddenly he got up and climbed over the rail on to the path.

"Come on, I'll walk you home."

* * *

A sharp breeze was picking up, whistling round the looming tower blocks. I pulled my jacket closely round me and looked up at the windows of the flats, imagining the lives lived in all those separate little boxes. For some people life was probably hell – drink, drugs and violence, part of the everyday scene; their small flat a prison. I was lucky. Although we'd had our bad times, Mum and Dad had never given up and they'd always been there for me, made me strong, made me believe in myself. I looked at Josh and wondered where he got his strength.

By the entrance to one of the blocks, I saw shadows stirring. Silent, dark figures. I moved a little closer to Josh.

"Sometimes this place gives me the creeps," I said.

Josh reached for my hand and I instantly felt more secure. He stroked my palm with his thumb, sending hot tingles shooting up my arm. I heard a low whistle.

"Hey, lover boy."

Josh pulled me close. "Just keep walkin'. Don't say anythin'."

"Who is it?" I whispered.

The whistle came again and we heard footsteps behind us.

"Yo, Josh . . . u . . . a, what ya doin' with Miss Bounty Bar?"

Josh pulled me along, quickening his pace. I heard a whirring noise and jumped as two bikes whizzed past. There was a squeal of brakes and mocking laughter spurted from the riders. We were trapped. Behind us – shadowy stalkers – and in front – cyclists, turning and heading straight for us.

Josh let go of my hand and thrust out his arm, barring their path. The bikes skidded to a halt. I recognized the cheeky grins of the cyclists and held my breath as Josh glared at them. Then, quick as lightning he spun round to face the figures behind.

"What do you want, Wes?" he demanded.

My breath came out in one long stream. Of course, it was Mabbott, who else would it be? Flanked by two heavies, he was waiting for us and when Josh spoke, he swaggered forward, hacked and spat.

"I wanna know what you doing wiv Miss Bounty Bar, Josh . . . u . . . a?"

Josh stood his ground, staring straight at him. "What you sayin', Wes?"

Wes puffed himself up, his shoulders widening to rhinoceros size. "I 'eard 'bout the band. I'm movin' to be your manager, but I don't want no Bounty Bar bitch in it."

He spat out the words, his fingers pointing for emphasis. I was ready to run but Josh seemed cool. He rolled his eyes, sighed and stepped forward. I held my breath as he stood directly in front of Wes.

"Wes, you know nothin' 'bout the band. Goldie, she the singer, without Goldie there ain't no band. You welcome to listen but it ain't your type of music."

I was sure Wes would thump him; certain he wouldn't stand for Josh speaking to him like that. He only had to reach out and he could smack Josh hard. But he didn't move.

For a few seconds it seemed as if we were all in a freeze frame, tension vibrating through the air. Then Wes pressed the forward button.

He stepped round Josh to glare at me. "You hear what I'm sayin'? She out of order," he said, pointing a big meaty finger in my direction.

I went cold, shivering as I crossed my arms; trembling fingers clutching at my jacket. Josh turned round to me as if he was going to say something, but then changed his mind and with a slight shrug of his shoulders, swung back to Wes.

"This band none of your business, Wes," he said, his voice strong and calm. "We musicians. We play what we want, with who we want." Then, he turned to me and put his arm round my shoulders. "Come on, Goldie. We're leavin'."

I was stunned. Surely Wes wouldn't let us walk away? I saw his bottom lip curl, his shoulders stiffen, but he made no move and Josh guided me away, towards the path which led home.

My eyes were round as saucers, my feet hardly touched the ground, my ears strained for the slightest sound – approaching footsteps or a sudden swish of anorak – but nobody came.

Josh didn't falter or speak until we reached the bridge. Then he stopped and let out a long low whistle. "Phew, that was close," he said.

"No kiddin'," I gasped. "But you were so cool."

He laughed softly. "I was bluffin'. Here, feel my heart."

He took hold of my hand and put it inside his jacket. I felt his heart beating fast.

"See? I'm no big-shot hero."

"You are to me," I said.

He dropped my hand and stood in front of me; his eyes looking into mine.

"I don't want you to be scared of Wes," he said softly. "I don't want you to be scared of anythin'. You're special, Goldie. Don't mind Wes – he just stupid."

"I know, but he's dangerous," I said. "He won't rest till he's split us up."

Josh stroked my cheek. "Don't worry. I can take care of Wes. All you got to do is sing. That's your job, right?"

He let go of me and looked away, pushing his dreadlocks back from his eyes. "Look, there's somethin' I haven't told you. I know Wes – known him since he was a baby. My mum used to mind 'im."

"Must have been a tough job," I said.

Josh closed his eyes for a moment, then he frowned and his face tightened into dark creases. When he spoke, his voice was jagged as broken glass.

"My mum was helpin' out – for the family. Wes is . . . my cousin. His dad . . . well – he my mum's brother."

I felt a real sense of shock. I was so surprised that I hardly heard what Josh said next but eventually his words filtered through my bewildered daze.

"Wes is wary of hurtin' me. If he do, he 'ave the whole family on his back. He know that." He took a deep breath, his shoulders heaving. "It was Wes and his dad who found my mum when she collapsed. They could have saved her."

I stood open-mouthed until the facts sunk in. "How can you ever talk to Wes?" I demanded.

My voice sounded sharp and angry and Josh moved away, scuffing his feet on the paving slabs. He thrust his hands deep into his pockets and stared into the distance. "It wasn't Wes, not really. He was just a kid, not old enough to be responsible. But his dad, he should 'ave phoned for the ambulance. He should 'ave done somethin'. But he was too stoned to think." He sighed and bit his lip. "Wes's dad is scum and Wes is going the same way."

"I'm sorry," I said. "That's horrible. I never knew Wes was your cousin."

Josh turned back to look at me; his eyes dark with pain. "Not something I brag about. You know what they say, you can choose your friends but you can't choose your relations."

I sagged against one of the bridge pillars; a dank, bitter smell wafted from the underpass. I felt sorry for Josh but somehow the news that he was Wes's cousin left me feeling more isolated. I heard Wes's voice in my head, "Bounty Bar". I knew what it meant. Black on the outside, white on the inside. I didn't belong anywhere. Josh had family, cousins, a whole tribe of them living on the estate, people I knew nothing about, but for me and my family there was nobody. We would go on being outsiders for ever.

I closed my eyes, sunk for a moment in despair, until a hand clasped my shoulder, shaking me gently. Suddenly Josh's face was close to mine.

"Hey! You gone off me now you know I'm related to Wes?"

"No," I gasped, caught off guard.

"Come here, then," he said.

I hesitated for the briefest second before I leant forward and collapsed against his chest. Through his thin T-shirt, I could hear his heart beating; feel the heat of his body. A soft wave of warmth washed through me, melting my tension, quelling my worries. I relaxed and felt safe.

"You not gonna worry no more? You promise?" Josh asked.

For an answer I rubbed my cheek against the hard boniness of his chest. I didn't care whose cousin he was, I wanted to kiss every bone in his body.

I felt his breath, hot on my face when he spoke. "Goldie, whatever happens I won't let Wes destroy the band," he said. "We won't give up on the music; it's our main hope."

He stroked my hair and neck and I sighed and nestled into his coat.

"I just wish Wes would leave us alone," I said.

Josh pulled away from me and looked into my eyes. "He like you, ya know."

"He's got a funny way of showing it."

"Yeah. I know but you . . . you . . . are. . ."

He paused and I looked up into his face.

"What am I?" I asked.

He didn't answer immediately. His forehead furrowed and his mouth pursed and puckered as if he was chewing on words he couldn't spit out. When he did speak his words came haltingly.

"Well . . . you . . . you. . ." He looked down at me, blinking, then he smiled and his face softened. "You're beautiful," he said.

And he leant forward and kissed me. It wasn't one of those really long, passionate, tongue-down-the-throat jobs, like I'd read about and seen on films. But it was a proper kiss. Slow and serious, deliberate and deep. And the best thing about it was that it was Josh doing it.

When he stopped, I clung to him for support because my body seemed to have turned to warm soup. I was breathing in short shallow gasps and my heart was thumping like a drum.

Josh kissed my neck, then he said in a sort of husky voice I didn't recognize, "I gotta go. I'm sorry, but my dad, he workin' late. I promise to make him somethin' to eat when he come in. An' I'm late. He might be home already."

Disappointment struck me like toothache but it lifted when he kissed me again. Behind my closed eyelids I saw bursting lights bright as a mirror ball and I went all trembly too; the whole bit, just like you're supposed to. I wanted the kiss to last and last but Josh broke away.

"You better go in," he whispered.

I nodded. I was too tingly to talk. As I watched Josh walk away, my body sang.

CHAPTER ELEVEN

When I woke next morning, my first thought was of Josh. He'd actually kissed me! A long, lingering, luscious kiss. Just thinking of it made me shudder with excitement. I wriggled my toes, drew up my knees and hugged my tummy, rocking back and forth under the warm blankets.

My bedroom window was brightening with early-morning sunshine and I stared at the temporary curtains Mum had tacked up, imagining that, beyond the window, under the bridge, over the concrete, Josh was lying in bed too, thinking about last night. Or at least I hoped he was.

I pictured the room I'd never seen. Dark walls covered with posters, his guitar propped in the corner. Discarded clothes lying on a chair. And what was he wearing? Pyjamas? No! T-shirt, boxer shorts. Nothing?!

Goldie Moon, you no good, girl, you'll come to a bad end having thoughts like that, I told myself. But I couldn't help it. My mind was replaying his kisses again – my body suffering minor earthquakes as I reconstructed every detail. His deep brown eyes beaming into mine, drawing closer; the curve of thick dark lashes as his eyes closed; the pressure of warm lips. My heart leapt like a basketball. Now I knew Josh fancied me!

I hoped I'd done it right. Hoped I was a good kisser. Wondered how I'd rate on those stupid one-to-ten scales in girls' magazines. Then decided I didn't care. Josh's kisses made me feel like my first single had got to number one. They were delicious, delectable, spine-tingling. I ran my tongue over my lips – I could still taste them.

I imagined Josh sleeping, dreaming about me. Eyes closed, matted dreadlocks rolling darkly over a pillow, light sculpting the fine curve of his cheekbone, an arm thrown out, dangling towards the floor, his strong fingers idle, delicate.

The image faded and questions boiled in my brain making me restless. Would Josh kiss me next time we met? Just like a natural hello kiss? And if he didn't – could I kiss him? Was I his girlfriend now? Thoughts of Josh overwhelmed me. Was I in love?

I will always love you. . .

The lyrics sang in my head . . . *I will always love. . .*

Yuk! that song was rubbish. Love was turning my brain to mush. I couldn't control myself. What I should be thinking about was all that scary stuff with Wes. How to prevent him interfering with the band, how to help Josh to control him. So, I'd talk to Josh, see Josh, kiss Josh? Goldie, will that help? Well, it might. Anyway, Josh was more intelligent, more sussed out than Wes would ever be. It was no competition.

I pictured Josh's face, his smile, his hands; saw him in the studio playing his guitar, a look of deep concentration on his face; fingers rippling over the strings. I remembered him looking at me with tenderness, heard his words – "You're beautiful."

I got out of bed and went over to the mirror, examining my face. Was I beautiful? My eyes gleamed back like two burning coals. My cheeks glowed, my mouth curved in a dreamy smile. Goldie, you look like some lovesick actor. You are out of control. Out of control and . . . loving it!

Everything would be just great if I could find a way to keep Wes off my back.

I danced into the bathroom and luxuriated in a deep foam-filled bath, dreaming of a future with Josh, star status with the band and of all the Sunday-morning baths I'd take without anybody hammering on the door to come in. . .

Bang, bang, bang. *Blast!* Bang, bang. *Damn!*

When I finally gave in, grabbed my bathrobe and opened the door, Patrick stood there clutching his stomach and looking a picture of woe.

"Why did you lock the door? I want to wee."

"Jeez, not chronic diarrhoea? Not violent vomiting?" I stepped aside, knotting my robe. "Come in, then, but hurry up."

Wrapping a towel round my wet hair, I waited whilst Patrick went to the loo, then sat on the bath and waited whilst he washed his hands. I wanted to put a face pack on and wished he'd hurry up but he seemed to be dawdling, scraping the soap over his fingernails and rubbing each finger in turn.

"Hurry up, Patrick."

He picked up a towel and turned towards me, his face furrowed by a deep frown. When he spoke, his voice was high and whining.

"Goldie, why does that big lad keep hangin' around? He frightens me."

My first stupid thought was that he meant Josh. As if Patrick was worried by Josh. He liked him. Then a sort of sickly fear took hold.

"Who do you mean?" I asked.

"That lad with the blond hair. Yesterday when I was playing with Dean and Chris, he kept flicking stones at us. And he called me nasty names and twice I seen 'im coming down 'ere and looking up at the house."

I bit my lip and sighed. Now Wraggy was starting on Patrick. And what was he watching our house for? That was creepy.

"Try to keep out of his way, Patti. He's a bully."

"I know. He come over and grabbed hold of me. Said I shouldn't be playin' with white kids. Said I was half-caste. He scares me."

His big brown eyes looked up, pleading for help; his body in his Superman pyjamas was thin and vulnerable. I imagined him scared witless by Andy Wragg – poor kid.

"I'll fix him, Patti," I said firmly. "Don't worry."

Patrick nodded. "Thanks, Goldie."

I felt a stab of guilt at his trust. Who did I think I was – Superwoman? No, as much as I liked to fight my own battles, I'd have to ask Josh to help me with this.

Leaving the house, I walked out across the open space towards the flats. As I passed the first block a door banged and two kids strode out, heads shaved, shoulders squared, hands in pockets, alert for trouble. They shouted to each other, their voices rasping with a bitter edge in the chilly morning air. One of them booted a stone, sending it bouncing over the concrete; the other vaulted a post then kicked at an empty can, swearing loudly. Was this how Patrick would turn out if we stayed here?

I scanned the flats. No sign of Josh, and when I took the long climb up to his flat, there was no answer. I ran down and carried on towards the square.

A woman, carrying a plastic bag, emerged from a shop doorway and headed towards me. At first I didn't recognize her because her head was a funny shape, a scarf covering a scalp full of bumpy rollers. Then I saw it was Mrs Potter, our next-door neighbour.

"'Eard you're singin' in a band," she said, stopping in front of me.

I shrugged my shoulders. I wasn't sure how to reply.

Her face puckered with disapproval. "Should 'ave thought you'd have better things to do," she said.

"It's for charity," I said, glaring at her.

"Oh." Her tongue made a soft clucking noise as she looked me up and down. Then she came closer. Her face pale as pummice stone, her lips thin and wet.

"You want to be careful. Look after that little bruvver of yours. I saw Andy Wragg twisting his arm up his back yesterday." She stood watching me, waiting to see if I looked suitably horrified. Then she shook her head. "Poor kid. He looked right upset."

I scowled. I knew she wasn't offering sympathy. She'd made her dislike of my family very obvious.

"Still, I expect he'll have to get used to it," she said sharply.

Alarm bells sounded in my head. "What do you mean?" I whispered.

She sucked in her lips as if tasting some foul medicine. "People like you," she said, "you don't belong, do yer?"

I stared at her, dumbfounded.

"Neither one thing nor the other. It's a shame but there it is. Always been the same 'ere. Folk looks after their own – black or white. It's those what's in-between as has a 'ard time."

I wanted to lash out at her, say something that would hurt her, make her feel ashamed. But anger was choking me.

"Never mind, love," she said as she walked off. "I expect you're used to it – people like you."

Thank you for those "kind" words, you nasty, ignorant woman, I thought. *It's people like you that make sure we don't belong. People like you who want to put people into boxes and make sure they stay there. One box for black and one for white. Don't you understand how blinkered that is? How it divides us all? We're all living on the estate, all trying to survive. Why can't we all live together in peace instead of hating each other?*

I stood, scuffing my shoes on the pavement. I was sick to death of all this racist stuff. All it did was cause hatred and violence. Desperately, I searched the square for Josh. Why wasn't he around when I needed him? Reluctantly, I headed home.

In the kitchen, Patrick seemed his usual chirpy self, eating Weetabix spread with large dollops of jam.

"Did you fix Wraggy?" he asked.

"It's not that easy. I didn't see him. Don't go playing too far from the house today. I'll talk to him tomorrow . . . at school."

"He doesn't go to school," Patrick said.

"Just shut up, Patti, or I won't fix it."

That sorted him. He went to ride his bike in front of the house. I spent most of my day trying to do science homework whilst hoping Josh would interrupt. But he didn't appear, and just as I was thinking of going to his flat again, Mum found me loads of jobs to do. Still, there was always rehearsal.

But that night, Josh didn't show. He'd never missed a band practice before. Something was wrong.

Tiger was a fury of activity, slamming and banging stuff about.

"Where's Josh?" I asked him.

"How the hell should I know?" he snapped, slamming a fist down on to the keyboard. Discordant notes sang in the air as I backed away.

"What's more, I don't care," he added.

My stomach tightened into a nervous knot. I glanced over at Nazim but he was beating the air with drumsticks and whistling under his breath.

The rehearsal was a disaster. My throat was tight and I couldn't sing properly. We didn't do any of Josh's songs and Nazim hardly said a word, drumming without enthusiasm and packing up early. I couldn't wait to leave and was about to disappear when Tiger shouted over to me.

"Hang on a minute, Goldie. I want a word."

I nodded and stood nervously biting my lip while he stashed his gear away.

"Let's go and get a coffee."

I followed him into the foyer, wondering what bombshell he was about to drop. Had Josh left the band? Was it finished?

Tiger bought two coffees and we sat facing each other across a low table. I waited for him to speak but his whole attention seemed to be concentrated on blowing the froth on his coffee. He said nothing and I began to get annoyed. After all, he was the one who'd asked me to wait. I'd just made up my mind to tell him this when he spoke.

"Me and Josh was up 'ere this mornin', 'avin a game of pool."

"Oh," I said, wondering what that had to do with anything.

He looked up. "Zoë asked us to do a gig, here at the Community Centre. It's been open thirty years – an anniversary, like."

My heart leapt. "But Tiger, that's brilliant," I said.

He frowned. "I told her, we don't want to be associated with nuffin' that's thirty years old. We today, man, we current, we not a sixties band."

"But it's a great venue. We'll have a proper stage, lighting. Better than some stuffy room in a pub."

His hands went up to adjust his baseball cap. "That's exactly what Josh said. You talk the same sort of shit as he does."

"Thanks," I said.

He sniffed. "Sorry, no offence. We just not ready." He blew on the foam again, sending a blob on to the table.

I thought of Josh squaring up to him, legs astride, chin jutting forward, a stance I'd seen before when he and Tiger clashed. My heart turned over.

I glanced at Tiger uneasily, wondering what to say. Words had to be chosen carefully.

He put down his drink and sat back, arms folded, a brooding look on his face. Then he sighed and some of the tension seemed to go out of his body. Leaning forward slightly, he said quietly, "I shouldn't have sounded off at him like I did."

He looked down at the table, concentrating hard, as his finger flicked at the spot of foam on the formica top. Then he continued: "He said I was scared and . . . I lost my temper, said stupid stuff about his songs . . . told him they were crap, had no bite . . . were bland . . . saccharine."

A faint blush of pink suffused his cheeks. No wonder Josh hadn't turned up!

After a few moments' silence I plucked up the courage to ask the million-dollar question.

"Are you scared of doing the gig?"

I could hardly believe I'd dared ask it, but he didn't shout at me – just looked even more embarrassed.

"I'm all right when I'm in the studio," he said. "I love it, it's great. I can make any sound I want, make it all work. But when you get out on stage . . . anything can happen."

"But we've been fine in rehearsals."

He shrugged. "I know, but it's not like the real thing. When you do a gig, you got to produce the goods. You got to do it on one particular night."

My jaw dropped. I was shocked. Tiger always seemed so confident, so sure of what he was doing.

"We can't just be a studio band, though," I said. "If we want to make it, we've got to perform."

His fingers tapped the edge of the table, and then he picked up his coffee. "Yeah, I know," he said. "It's just that everybody who comes to a gig at the Centre . . . they'll know us."

I stared down at the table, thinking hard.

"We might not be able to do the concert anyway," I said. "Wes is making trouble. Last night he was going on about wanting to manage the band and saying he wanted me out."

Tiger put his coffee down and stared at me. "What? What the hell's his problem? The band's nothin' to do with him."

"He thinks it is."

"You're jokin'," Tiger said.

I shook my head. "No, he was deadly serious."

Tiger leant back and cracked his knuckles. "I get it. He's jealous. He can't bear anything happenin' on the estate that he doesn't control."

I nodded. "Yes, and he hates me."

Tiger clasped his hands, his chin jutted forward and his usual air of confidence returned. "Well, nobody's gonna tell me what to do," he said firmly. "And nobody's gonna dictate who's in my band. We'll all do the gig and we'll be bloody brilliant."

I smiled at him – my plan had worked. I put my hand on his. "Thanks, Tiger. I feel the same way. We've got to fight Wes. We'll work so hard the gig will be a roaring success . . . everybody will love us and then he'll have to back off. It'll be fantastic."

He hesitated, looking doubtful again. "Yeah, maybe," he said uncertainly.

I grasped his hand. "Come on, Tiger, I know how you feel but what about me? It's a much bigger risk for me. Wes is gunning for me. I need your support."

He sat for a moment, head down, silently contemplating. I held my breath. Then he looked up. "OK," he said. "You've got it. I'll tell Zoë we'll do the gig."

As we stood up, Tiger patted my shoulder. "You're not bad for a singer, yer know," he said with a grin.

We walked out into the dark square.

"You gonna be OK?" he asked.

I caught sight of a tall shadow waiting by the shops.

I smiled and met Tiger's eyes. "Yeah, I'll be fine."

CHAPTER TWELVE

As Tiger walked away I headed across the square, my heart thudding in anticipation. I couldn't wait to tell Josh that Tiger would do the gig. But when I reached the shops, the tall shadow I'd seen seemed to have melted away. The square was empty. There was no sign of anyone – no Josh.

An uneasy quiet settled around me, as if the darkness was hiding something. In the distance, a shrill cry rose, but was quickly sucked away by the cool night air. I began to feel nervous and moved into the lamplight. Better get home, I decided. I'd been mistaken, Josh wasn't going to show.

Keeping to the middle of the path, I started for home. Suddenly, the square was filled with the sound of running footsteps. A tall, lanky figure silhouetted against the yellow glare of street lamps was racing towards me. My heart jumped.

"Josh," I whispered.

But as the figure came closer I saw it wasn't Josh. It was someone with cropped hair, someone white.

He was running fast, veering to left and right as if unsure which way to go. Snorting like a runaway horse, he ran round in a circle then turned and raced towards the shelter of the shops at the bottom end of the square. Almost immediately, his pursuers, a gang of lads, streamed round the corner. Somebody yelled and they ran after the lone youth, disappearing into the shadowy darkness.

I heard them chasing and shouting. Then there was an excited yell and scuffling sounds. Shouts and swearing filled the night air, and then, in the settling silence, I heard a gasp and a horrible low moan.

I shuddered with fear as I peered into the darkness. I heard more cries and then groaning. I knew someone was in deep trouble but I was too afraid to help.

Slowly and carefully, I took a few steps forward. A lamp glared in my eyes and all I could make out were shadows. There were several people crouching, huddled close to the ground. I stared at them, trying to understand what was happening.

Then I heard a sharp voice shout, "Hey, look, somebody watchin' us."

One of the shadows detached itself, moved towards me – dark and bulky. Even before I could make out his features, I knew it was Wes.

"Hey, if it ain't Goldie Moon," he said, his voice soft as butter.

I stared into the dark shadow of his face, caught the smell of his smoky breath as he bent forward, then I trembled as he reached out and grasped the edge of my shirt.

"Bit late for you to be out on your own, isn't it?"

He held me fast. I didn't struggle; I knew it was useless. "I'm just going home," I said and was amazed at how calm my voice sounded.

He marched me forward into the glow of the lamp. His face was set in a manic grin and I noticed the small deep scar on his upper lip.

"Going home?" he repeated.

"Yes," I said, my voice quivering now.

"Oh . . . ain't that sweet . . . lucky girl. Back to that nice little house, those pretty flowers and that cute baby brother."

I jerked back. "You leave my brother alone."

"Now, now. Don't go gettin' all upset. You say nothin' about seein' us here and your brother and your family be safe."

I heard the soft rustle of his leather coat, felt a rough hand on my arm, then he grabbed me round the waist, his breath hot on my neck. "Got you now."

I kicked out, trying to free myself, but his arms were like a tight metal band round my middle and he laughed as he lifted me off my feet. I squirmed and kicked, wriggling sideways, ramming my shoulders into his ribs, but he just squeezed harder. As my head rolled forward, I gasped for breath and saw something that made me lose all hope of escape. In his hand was a knife, the long blade smeared with blood.

I trembled violently, then went limp. When he let go of me, I dropped heavily to the floor, lurching sideways. He grabbed a handful of my hair and twisted me round until I was facing him. The pain in my head made me want to scream.

"Not so fast. You seen nothin' 'ere tonight. Know what I'm sayin'?"

Speechless with fear, I nodded. The knife blade flashed in front of my eyes, centimetres away from my face.

"You tell the cops that you seen me and you're dead," he said. Then he leant forward, stretched out his hand and slowly wiped the blade across the sleeve of my coat. A gleaming stripe smeared the dark material. I stared at it, mesmerized, until he pushed me hard and I lost my balance, staggering sideways and crashing on to the concrete.

"Think you so sassy. You nothin', girl. Nothin'," he snarled.

I lay for a moment, unable to move. My elbow felt like it was on fire. I tried to calm myself, breathing slowly and deeply, but I couldn't stop shivering. I closed my eyes, hoping he'd go away.

For a few moments everything was quiet. Had he gone? I hadn't heard him walk away. I chanced opening my eyes, blinked in the glare of the street lamp and raised my head. He was standing a little way off, his head up, alert, listening.

Tentatively I rolled on to my side as footsteps drummed towards me, shaking the ground. The gang came streaming across the square, snorting like wild animals. They stopped, sniffing the air as if wondering which way to go. Then I heard a cry.

"The cops. Run!"

Wes's body jerked like a mad thing, twitching and turning. He gasped, lunged sideways towards some bushes, hesitated for a moment, one arm raised in the air, then he bolted.

Somehow I managed to roll on to my knees and pull myself up, my head reeling, bile rising to my throat. I couldn't run, I could hardly walk, but I managed to stagger a few steps.

When I heard a police siren I dragged myself over the rough wooden rail that divided the path from the bushes. I heard shouts. In the distance a blue light flashed. I prayed the police had caught Wes, hoped they'd come and find the lad who was hurt.

I heard a shout and hurrying footsteps. "Here, over here!"

They'd found the boy. I hoped it wasn't too late. I imagined him lying there on the cold hard ground, blood seeping from his wound, thick dark blood forming a pool. My stomach heaved itself into my mouth and I bent over and vomited on to the grass.

I waited a few moments, breathing deeply, steadying myself on the rail, then I felt in my pocket, found a scrappy tissue and wiped my mouth.

I looked around. The square was empty now and a soft rain made the lamps hazy. I leant forward, squinting into the shadowy cluster of leaves and branches. All I saw were squashed drink cans and ring pulls glinting in yellow light. But it had to be there – I was sure I'd seen Wes throw away the knife.

I inched along the rail, my shadow making dark patches even darker. I scraped my foot over the ground, nervously exploring. At the other side of the bush, a glimmer of metal deep in the branches caught my eye.

My heart pumped as I dropped to my knees, then, hardly daring to breathe, I slid forward. Turning my head from the prodding twigs I reached into the leaves and my hand touched something hard. I tried to grasp it but it slid away. Raising my head, I peered into the network of branches. Yes, it was still there. If I lay down and stretched. . . Ah. Success. I grasped the handle and drew out the knife.

I held it, steel sharp and stained, up to the light. Wes's knife. A few minutes ago, I'd feared it, but now it was mine. As I stared at the blade, I felt a surge of power.

The next moment I heard sudden, heavy footsteps behind me. I jumped and shrank into the shadow of the bushes, peering out across the square. Somebody was walking towards me.

"All quiet now. Whoever was here is long gone," a deep voice said.

It was the police. Two of them searching the square. I watched and waited, the knife handle burning into the palm of my hand.

Here's the knife. I've got the knife that stabbed him.

The words rang in my head, formed in my throat, but they were left unsaid. I saw the murderous glint in Wes's eyes and the words shrivelled and died. Who'd protect my family? Who'd protect me? I knew what Wes was capable of.

One of the men came close. I saw the pale moon of his face under the lamp as I crouched trembling.

Goldie. Be brave. Do the right thing.

I can't. Wes will destroy me – it's suicide.

Goldie. Give up the knife. What if the boy dies? You can't let Wes get away with murder.

The policeman stood, head cocked, watching and listening, then he coughed and walked away.

You can't let this happen.

But I did. I opened my mouth to shout after him but no words came. Then I turned, raised my hand and hurled the knife back into the bushes. And suddenly I was running, running as fast as I could and I didn't stop or look back until I reached home.

CHAPTER THIRTEEN

Hot news sizzled on everybody's lips as I entered the classroom next day.

"Andy Wragg's been stabbed . . . he's in intensive care . . . had a blood transfusion . . . needed ten litres."

I pieced together the story, spinning round like a dizzy doll, turning to hear first one person and then another.

"They say he's critical."

"I 'eard he was stabbed in the ribs. That's near your heart, innit?"

"He lost loads of blood. It was all over the shop doorway."

"He might die."

There was a general gasp of horror. Then a ginger-haired lad started laughing, actually laughing, his face blushing red, fluorescent light glinting off his glasses.

"Knew somethin' like this would 'appen to 'im . . . he was 'eadin' for it . . . stupid dickhead . . . gettin' careless, thought he was friggin' invincible. Now he goes and gets 'imself stabbed."

I moved to the edge of the group, feeling sick and shaky. So it was Andy Wragg I'd seen last night, running in the lamplight, running for his life.

I shivered as I remembered the dark smear of blood on my jacket. This morning it had dried and was hardly visible on the black material. Nobody would know it had been there . . . except Wes . . . except me.

My arm was jogged and I turned to find Miranda, cheeks pink and shiny, eyes agog.

"Terrible, innit? He lives not far from me."

She'd hardly spoken to me since flouncing out of my bedroom but now she clutched my arm like she was my best friend and steered me away from the crowd. I didn't mind; I couldn't stand their gloating and wallowing.

"It makes me sick," I said. "They're talking like it's some episode of *EastEnders*. But it's not – it's real. Poor lad."

Miranda's eyebrows shot up in surprise. "Do you know Andy Wragg?"

"I've seen him."

She looked puzzled for a moment then nodded her head. "Yeah, I know what yer mean. They think it's like dead excitin' but it's Charlene's bruvver. She'll be real cut up about it." Leaning close, she dropped her voice. "Makes you feel weird though, don't it? I went to see Gran last night, walked right past them shops. Could have been 'appenin' then, couldn't it?"

I was silent, biting my lip, haunted by scenes from last night, hearing again that terrible moan.

Miranda touched my shoulder. "What's wrong? You look terrible, like someone just put a knife in you."

I blinked, my head full of swirling pictures: a tall, lanky boy running; crouching figures huddled close to the ground; the glint of the knife in Wes's hand.

"I . . . I was in the square . . . last night," I stuttered.

The words were out before I had time to consider.

Miranda's mouth gasped open. "Where? What did you see?"

I hesitated. No. Not Miranda. Don't tell Miranda. It was like a warning siren going off in my head. Desperately, I looked round for Josh. The room swung crazily, chairs and tables spinning. I swayed towards Miranda and she steadied me, putting her arm round my shoulders.

"Gawd, you look awful. Come on."

She led me to a table near the wall and sat me down. My head lolled forwards and crimson light danced across my eyelids like splashed blood.

Miranda shook me gently. "Come on, get it off yer chest. You can tell me," she urged.

I blinked and swallowed hard.

"Goldie. Did you see anyfin' last night?"

"No," I whispered.

"Goldie," she squeaked. "You did. I can tell you did. It's written all over your face."

I glanced anxiously at the group of gossipers, not wanting draw their attention. "I just thought I heard something after rehearsal, that's all," I said quietly.

"You saw Wraggy, didn't yer?"

I looked down, saying nothing.

Miranda moved so that her head was almost on my shoulder, her hair touching mine. "Did you see 'em fightin'?" She sniffed. "Come on, you can trust me. I won't tell nobody. I swear."

Her eyes were glued to my face, reading my expression. She was willing me to confide in her. "You'll feel better if you tell somebody," she encouraged.

"I won't," I whispered.

"You saw Wes, didn't yer?" she asked.

I said nothing but when I glanced up, I saw her eyes widen to dinner plates as if I'd told her some vital news. Then her eyes narrowed. "It was Wes, wasn't it?" she said. "He was there. You saw 'im, didn't yer? Was he wiv his gang?"

'I couldn't see anything properly. It was dark," I said.

Miranda gripped my arm. "Everybody knows Wes was out to get Wraggy. If you saw Wes there, you got to tell."

"I didn't see anything," I protested.

Her face was eager, mouth gaping. "You gotta tell what you saw."

"Look, I don't want any trouble," I said.

But Miranda was away now, letting her mind run riot. "Always knew Wes would do somethin' stupid one day. He's a lunatic, 'e needs lockin' up. You should go to the police."

"Look, I told you, I know nothing," I said nervously.

"Oh, yes you do!" she snapped. "It's just that yer don't want to tell me. You don't wanna trust yer best mate."

And with that she looked quickly away, focusing on the

group of people who were still gossiping. When she turned back to me she had a certain, confident look about her as if she'd made her mind up.

"I think you should go and tell Mrs Newman what you saw," she said. "She'll inform the police."

I bit my thumbnail and sighed. I knew she was right but I couldn't risk it.

Pulling my arm free, I said quietly but firmly, "No, there's nothing to tell."

I got up and started to walk away but she followed me, whispering urgently in my ear.

"Goldie, you could sort Wes. Fix 'im so he can't bother you no more."

I turned on her. "You've changed your tune. Last week you wanted me to go out with him," I said.

She raised her eyebrows. "Yeah, well that was before he half-murdered somebody."

I wanted her to go away now. I wished I'd said nothing to alert her. "I'm going to see Josh," I said.

Her lip curled spitefully. "Oh yeah, talk to Josh. Mister friggin' wonderful. Don't take any notice of what I say. All I know is, if yer don't act quickly you'll lose yer chance and Josh ain't no match for Wes. I can tell you that fer nothin'. 'E can't protect yer."

"What do you know?" I snapped.

She smiled smugly. "I know what Wes is capable of. An' Josh is too soft," she said.

I wanted to hit her. I clenched my fists, gritted my teeth and stared at her, my eyes sparking with fury. Josh would fight for me, I knew he would. He'd stand up to Wes for me. But I also knew I didn't want him to have to. I didn't want to give Wes Mabbott a reason to come after any of us, not me or Patrick, nor Mum or Dad . . . or Josh.

But Miranda didn't care. She was still trying to persuade me. Leaning close, she hissed in my ear, "Josh don't have the answer to the bleedin' universe, yer know. If you listen to me you can nail Wes then he won't bother you no more. If he's banged up. He won't bother none of us."

She waited a moment but when I didn't say anything, she rocked back on her heels, gave me a cold, hard stare and pushed past me, returning to the crowd of gloaters who were still milking the drama for all it was worth.

With a sinking heart I watched as she smiled and linked arms with a tough-looking, dark-haired girl. It was Nicola, Charlene Wragg's best friend. I sat down at a table, pretending to sort out my books whilst inwardly cursing myself. I should have denied ever being in the square, said something to put her off the scent – I knew how she gossiped.

When somebody in the group gasped loudly I glanced over and caught Miranda's eye. She stared back defiantly.

"Yeah, Charlene will be beside 'erself," I heard her say loudly. But somehow I knew that wasn't who she'd been talking about.

The bell went for morning lessons and people began to

gather their stuff and troop out. I picked up my bag and headed for the door, but as I was leaving I locked eyes with Miranda.

During first lesson, I found it impossible to concentrate. My fingers tightened on my pen as I remembered the clutch of Wes's fingers on my neck, his hand on my shirt, the terror I'd felt when I saw the knife. I rubbed at my sore elbow, wondering what it had been like for Andy Wragg. Had he seen his attackers? Did he feel the knife going in? And then, with a shudder, I remembered – last night, holding the knife. Had they found it?

When break came I slowly made my way back to the form room keeping a wary eye peeled for Wes. If Miranda was doing what I thought she was doing, plus throwing in a few added details, then it wouldn't be long before he came looking for me.

Sitting down at a table against the wall I stuffed my oversized school bag in front of my face and shrank down behind it, making myself as small as possible. I rested my head on the bag, ignoring everyone, making it clear that I wanted to be left alone. When someone prodded my shoulder I jumped like I'd been scalded. Then with a tremendous surge of relief I saw it was Josh. He sat down beside me and took my hand; his lovely face creased with worry lines, his eyes haunted.

"Goldie, I been so worried 'bout you. Everybody's sayin'

you in trouble. They say you was in the square last night when Wraggy was stabbed."

"Who said that?" I asked.

"Miranda."

Differing emotions fought for control. I was furious with Miranda for spreading gossip but I couldn't help feeling a tingle of excitement when I saw how anxious Josh looked. His eyes were eating me up, making sure I was OK. Gratefully, I leant against him, snuggling my head on to his shoulder.

"I saw Mabbott with a knife," I said, tears pricking my eyes.

Josh stroked my hair. "Oh, shit," he breathed.

"I know. I'm in it up to my neck," I said, tears welling in my eyes.

"Hey, don't cry. We just gotta think what to do," Josh said.

I could feel people watching us. I sniffed, dashing the tears away with the back of my hand.

"Here," Josh said, handing me a neatly folded tissue. Then he wrapped his arms around me, shielding me from view. "Did you see Wraggy get stabbed?" he whispered.

"No," I said. "It was dark. I saw somebody on the ground but I didn't know who it was. Then Wes came for me and he had a knife . . . and. . ."

I couldn't speak as the horror of last night closed in again. Josh's arms tightened round me.

"I won't let anythin' 'appen to you," he said softly.

Somebody whistled at us but it didn't matter. I nestled close to Josh, allowing his words to soothe me. I sighed, wiped my eyes and let myself, just for a moment, believe everything would be all right. Then, as I shifted slightly, I saw a shadow. Wes stood over us, his maroon blazer like a bloodstain against the light.

He stepped forward and tapped Josh on the shoulder. "Yo, sorry to break up this little love nest but I got some business."

Josh's arms loosened, he let go of me and stood up.

"What do you want?" he asked.

Wes smiled, a crooked snarl of a smile. "I got no business wiv you. It's Miss cock-teaser 'ere I want to see."

I hoped Josh wouldn't make an issue of what Wes had called me. They were just words. I could stand that. I got up and faced Wes across the table.

"You want to talk to me?" I asked, in the boldest voice I could muster.

"Yeah . . . in private."

The air was electric, I felt Josh was about to explode and I knew I had to get Wes away from him. Angry as he was, I didn't fancy Josh's chances against Wes's muscular bulk. So, as calmly as I could, I took Josh's hand and told him, "Stay here. I'll be OK, it's just a little matter Wes and I have to sort out."

Josh stepped forward, glaring down at Wes. "You better not touch her," he said, and his voice had an edge that was razor sharp.

I saw Wes's shoulders tense. In another moment he'd take Josh. Swiftly, I moved round the table and placed a firm hand on Wes's arm.

"We can talk outside," I said, managing to keep my voice steady.

Amazingly, Wes allowed me to lead him out of the classroom. I walked slowly, wondering if I was being extremely stupid. The people we passed were silent, awed, waiting for the explosion.

Just past our classroom the corridor came to a dead end. No escape. The tiles were grubby, paint flaking from the walls. I stopped and turned, trying to stand as tall and straight as I could, because, although he was twice my width, Wes was only my height and I could look him straight in the eye.

Blood throbbed in my ears as he stared back at me but then his gaze flickered and he glanced away. His eyes flashed down to the floor then to the side, his tongue flicked out then jammed sideways into the corner of his mouth. Suddenly I saw he was scared. He was as nervous as I was. What I knew was a threat. Buoyed up by this discovery, I spoke first, asking in a clear, firm voice what he wanted.

He looked at me under lowered lashes, then leant forward. "Thought I told you to keep quiet about last night. Tell nobody." He raised a fist and prodded the air with a giant finger. "People are talkin'. Did you grass on us?"

I glared at him, keeping my gaze as steady as I could.

My silence made him angry and his voice was louder now, sharp and urgent. "Anythin' 'appen to me an' I'll hold you responsible. You know what I'm sayin'?"

My gaze didn't flicker. I refused to be intimidated because I knew if I acted like a victim, I'd become one.

"I'm not responsible for your actions," I said defiantly, staring straight at him.

Wes gulped, his face tightened into mean, ugly lines. He glanced around, his eyes darting anxiously as if looking for someone, afraid we were being watched and overheard. Then he leant closer.

"You know whose side you on, girl. You black, you know that, you got niggers' blood. And us black brothers, we stick together. No shit. You get ma meanin'?"

Then he loomed over me, his thick jaw set solid as rock, his huge clenched fist in front of my face.

I steeled myself to stare him out. "I'm not black," I said. "I'm a Bounty Bar."

Wes moved his fist closer to my face. "You think you clever. But, if I find out you been spreading gossip then you and your family are dead meat. Understand?"

His tone was so full of venom that it made me tremble. He sounded as if he'd kill us all. But even as his words sunk in, I seethed with anger. Now he was pulling all this black brother stuff. Now it was convenient for me to be black. Two days ago I was a Bounty Bar.

"You'd better make your mind up what I am. But I don't

care if I'm black, white, yellow or red. I'm me, Goldie Moon, and what I know could get you into big trouble."

Raising my head, I focused my eyes on him and pressed home my advantage. "You better keep away from my family if you know what's good for you. I've got evidence could put you in jail."

I saw him flinch and his fist rise. I dodged to one side.

"What you mean?" he demanded.

I took a chance. "You should be more careful where you drop your rubbish." I said. "Keep away from me or I'll take my evidence to the police."

He stared at me, his eyes like laser beams, piercing my soul but I didn't care.

"You can't prove nothin'," he spluttered.

"If you've got a clear conscience, you've got nothing to worry about, have you?" I said.

And I turned and walked past him.

Josh and some others were standing a little way off, watching and waiting. The few steps it took me to reach them seemed to take for ever. Any moment I expected to be grabbed from behind. I never thought Wes would let me walk away. But he did.

Josh put his arm round me and we pushed our way through the others and walked down the corridor.

Inside an empty classroom I leant against Josh, shuddering whilst tears ran down my face.

"I hate Wes Mabbott," I said.

His arm tightened around my shoulders.

"Goldie, you crazy. My heart was beatin' for ya. What did you tell 'im?"

"He thinks . . . I've got his knife," I sobbed.

Josh eyes widened. "How?" he asked.

"He . . . dropped it when he heard the police coming and I picked it up. I thought. . ." I struggled to control my voice. "I'm not sure what I thought. Perhaps I was going to give it to the police, perhaps I thought I could keep it and then Wes wouldn't dare touch me. I don't know – it's all so confused."

I sniffed, brushing away my rolling tears. Josh pulled me to him, stroking my hair and patting my back. I sobbed into his shirt and he let me cry, making soothing noises and wiping away the occasional tear with the sleeve of his blazer.

When I'd stopped crying he lifted my face and wiped it with his tie.

"You're soaking wet," I said. "I'm sorry."

"Don't worry," he said. "Anyway, some of this my fault. If I'd been at rehearsal last night, none of this would have happened."

"I thought you were waiting for me," I said. "I thought I saw you but it wasn't you. It must have been Andy Wragg."

Josh hugged me and kissed my cheek. "Look, we'll beat this thing. You more clever than Wes. You already got one up on him. He thinks you got the knife, so he's scared. He'll lie low and that'll buy us some time. Then, we've got to think what to do."

I shook my head. "I can't think. I'm so frightened."

We were quiet for a few moments, me resting my head on Josh's chest, listening to his breathing. I knew he was trying to figure out how to help me and I loved him for it, but I couldn't imagine what we could do. If Wes found out I didn't have the knife after all – I was for it.

Suddenly Josh's head jerked up. "We've got to get the knife back," he said. "Find it before the police or anybody else. Then we really will have something to bargain with."

"OK," I agreed, although I couldn't bear the thought of ever seeing the knife again.

We slipped out of school at lunch time and I imagined we were being watched; undercover police officers or Wes's gang hiding behind hedges, spying on us. I walked fast, wondering if we were walking into a trap and if we were, I wanted it all to be over quickly.

When we reached the square we saw two police officers in uniform talking to some shoppers. We kept our eyes on them as we skirted round the far side of the square and squeezed through the undergrowth.

"What if they see us?" I worried.

"They're too busy questioning people to notice us," Josh reassured me.

I wasn't convinced. My mouth was dry and my heart

thumped fast as we pushed our way through to the far path. I looked over at the bushes remembering how I'd scrabbled frantically to find the knife, then thrown it away in panic.

"There," I pointed. "In that bush."

We edged forward, my eyes searching the ground. I saw tin cans, plastic bags, cigarette packets – but there was no knife. It had gone.

CHAPTER FOURTEEN

A few days later, I stood with the rest of my tutor group as a plain clothes policewoman, Detective Inspector somebody, addressed us.

". . .a serious offence, stabbing took place, nobody's coming forward with information, somebody could have died . . . somebody might have witnessed . . . we think somebody knows who was responsible . . . we need evidence . . . somebody. . ."

I closed my ears. I didn't need more details. I knew. Icy fingers crept up and down my spine. I pushed my hands deep down into my blazer pockets, tensing my arms, clenching my teeth, trying to stop myself from shivering. Around me I heard whispers. In front of me I saw Miranda's blonde head. Would she give me away?

I looked down at the floor, closed my eyes and heard Gran's voice. Clear and musical, it rang through my head.

"Goldie, you gotta do the right thing. Goldie, you gotta stand up for right."

I turned, searching for her face, almost convinced she was standing beside me, but all I saw were two sharp, glittering splinters, chips of black ice. Over the heads of two smaller pupils, Wes was staring right at me.

Quickly I looked away. There were rows of kids in front, tall, short, broad; blonde bob, brown ponytail, black corn-rowed. My gaze darted along the backs of heads, looking for Josh. I heard another voice, a strong male voice. I glanced up at the stage and saw a tall, thin man speaking.

"We'll be in the head's office all afternoon, if anyone wants to talk to us. All information is welcome. Everything told to us will be treated with the strictest confidence . . . any detail, no matter how small. . ."

My heart raced and I felt myself sway. I dug my fingernails into the palms of my hands. *Stay in control, Goldie. Don't draw attention to yourself.*

Pupils were turning and shuffling. I heard my name. Somebody whispered it, then I heard it repeated. One thought filled my mind. I had to escape, I just had to.

The line in front began to move and I saw Josh waiting near the door. I pushed forward, side-stepped, squeezed between people, weaving my way through to him.

"There's no rush," a teacher barked. "Anybody'd think you wanted to get to lessons."

I thought he might stop me but he didn't and I carried on weaving and dodging until I was beside Josh.

"Don't worry none," he whispered, as he grabbed my hand.

I waited till we were clear of the hall, then I said urgently, "I've got to leave. I can't stay in school. I've got to get away."

Josh didn't hesitate. "All right. I'll come with you."

As pupils streamed by, we dodged into one of the music-practice rooms, waited – silent and breathless – then, when it was clear, we slipped out of a side door.

Neither of us had played truant before, and we tried telling each other it was fun. We walked down the high street and went into McDonald's. Between us we managed to scrape up enough money for a milkshake and fries, but as we sat at the yellow plastic table we couldn't relax. We were out of place amongst the pushchairs and ketchup-mouthed toddlers. Women balancing trays above bags of shopping eyed us suspiciously and I kept glancing over to the door, imagining Wes or Ralph might come after us. Then, when I saw somebody who looked like Mum I got paranoid and thought we'd been spotted. I hurried Josh outside but couldn't think where to go. Josh's flat was out of the question because his dad was sick and I didn't dare go to my house.

In driving rain we sheltered in shop doorways, but our school uniforms made us conspicuous. A salesman asked us what we were doing out of school.

It was Josh who came up with the idea of going to the Community Centre. We walked there the long way round so we didn't have to go past school and we were cold and wet when we stumbled into the foyer.

Zoë was filling the chocolate machine and looked round when she heard the door. When she saw it was us, she smiled, as if it was the most natural thing for us to call at two o'clock on a Wednesday afternoon.

"Hi! Hoped you two might drop in. 'Ow's it going?"

We stood there shivering.

"Oooh, you look like two drowned cats. Come and have a cup of coffee and some choccy." She picked up a handful of Mars bars and closed the door of the machine. "Hey, an' I can show you the posters. I've just printed them."

We followed her into the office.

"Over there," she pointed, as she went to pour coffee.

I looked down at a pile of bright posters. Bold black lettering jumped up at me:

> Get back to your roots
> Be where it's cool
> NO FEAR
> Saturday June 10th 7.30 p.m.

As I read, my stomach contracted. I'd been so preoccupied with Wes Mabbott and the web of trouble he created, that I'd almost forgotten the gig. Now, suddenly, it became real. It hit me like a crashing wave. I'd be up there on stage with a live audience watching and listening. Mum, Dad, Nancy, Miranda, everybody and anybody from the estate – Ralph, Wes, Wraggy.

"Oh, my God," I said. "They could eat us alive."

Zoë laughed. "Don't be a wally. You're fantastic, brilliant. Don't forget, I've heard you sing and the band's spot on."

"Yeah. But we really got to put some 'ard work in now," Josh said.

I nodded in agreement but I wasn't thinking about rehearsing, I was remembering Wes's words. "I'm movin' to be your manager but I don't want no Bounty Bar bitch in my band."

Zoë must have seen the worried look on my face. "They'll think you're great," she reassured me. "You'll have them queuing up for your autograph. Eh, an' it's time something good happened in this place. We've had some rotten stuff goin' on lately."

She handed us mugs of coffee.

"The fuzz came round yesterday. Actin' all friendly, wantin' some help. Said Andy Wragg was friggin' lucky to survive. They want to nail somebody but nobody's talkin'."

She threw a chocolate wrapper in the bin then turned to look at me. "If I knew who did it, I'd tell. I couldn't rest till he was locked up."

I perched on the edge of the desk and looked down, avoiding Zoë's gaze. My finger traced the little heart that Josh had drawn on my school bag.

"Next time he could kill somebody," Zoë said, quietly.

Her words gave me a jolt like an electric shock. I felt so bad I wanted to crawl under the desk. Guilt oozed from every pore.

There was an uncomfortable silence then Josh broke in. "We've gotta go."

"But you haven't drunk your coffee yet," Zoë protested.

Josh apologized. "Sorry, I jus' remembered. We gotta get back to school. We only just passin'. Glad we did, though, the posters are great."

"Thanks," Zoë said. Then, reaching into a drawer, she pulled out some tickets. "Can you sell some?"

Josh stretched out his hand. "Yeah, sure."

As I got up to go, Zoë came round the desk and put her hand on my shoulder. "Look, I'm always here if you want to talk," she said. "I know it can be tough just tryin' to survive in this place."

I nodded. "Yeah."

"I'm really pleased the band is working out for you. I want this gig to be the best. I don't want anythin' to ruin it," she said. Then her eyes met mine. "You are good, you know," she added.

"Thanks," I said.

Josh caught my arm and hurried me out.

"Come on," he whispered.

I knew Josh was trying to protect me but I couldn't hurry. Zoë's last words rang in my ears. The words had a double meaning. Yes, she meant the band was good but it was also an appeal to my better nature. She'd heard the gossip – she was asking me to grass on Mabbott.

"She knows," I said.

"What?"

"Oh, Josh."

"How can she know?"

I looked down at the ground, biting my lip. "Miranda. Good old Miranda spreading the gossip."

Josh put his arm round me. "Look, all you know is Wes was there. OK, you saw 'im with a knife, but that don't prove nothin'. They probably all had blades."

I blinked, trying not to cry, then I looked up, tears welling in my eyes. "Josh, Wes's knife had blood on it. I know he stabbed Wraggy."

I saw Josh wince and heard him sigh. I hesitated for a second then carried on. "Somebody must have found the knife. Maybe Wes went back and found it before we did."

Josh's face tightened into dark creases. "No. Wes is still scared. I saw his face when the police were talking. He was watching you real close."

"I should have done the right thing, handed the knife to the police in the first place," I said. "But it's not too late, is it? I could tell them what I saw."

I waited for Josh to answer, to tell me what to do, but he didn't say anything. I caught his hand, slid my fingers between his and silently pleaded with him – *don't leave me, Josh, I can't do this on my own.*

His mouth puckered and he frowned in concentration. I could almost hear him turning things over in his mind, then he spoke. "I don't know Goldie. No one on this estate like the police."

I stared at him a moment. Was he scared for me or for

himself? I sighed. *Damn*. This whole nightmare was poisoning my brain – now I was even beginning to doubt Josh.

I laid my head on his shoulder, my mind full of clashing arguments. If I turned informer I'd be ostracized, my family a target for hatred – Mabbott's mob would destroy us. But how could I go on with my life, hold my head up and sing at the concert, knowing I was shielding a criminal? Oh, I wished I'd never been in the square that night, I was so sick and tired of it all.

Josh touched my hair, I felt his breath on my neck. "You gotta be real careful, Goldie. I don't know Wes any more. He's dangerous."

I leant against him, thinking deeply, then I made up my mind. I was a singer, a performer, not a bloody crusader. Why should I jeopardize my career just to put Wes Mabbott away for a few years?

I lifted my head and smiled at Josh. "Sod Wes Mabbott, I'm going to concentrate on rehearsing – we've got to make the concert brilliant. I want us to be fantastic, I want success."

CHAPTER FIFTEEN

For the next few days I didn't see Wes Mabbott and I tried to push all thought of stabbings and knives, violence and victims to the back of my mind. Josh organized lots of rehearsals, so I was kept busy. When I crossed the estate I kept a wary eye out for Wes or his cronies but I walked unharmed.

At school, I listened for news of Andy Wragg, hoping desperately that he'd recover, hoping I hadn't witnessed a murder. Rumours spread and multiplied. He was dying; scarred for life; then I heard he was out of hospital, back on the streets and looking for revenge.

Even Josh couldn't seem to find out the truth. Charlene wasn't back at school, so we couldn't ask her, and none of Wraggy's gang were talking. I imagined that was the way Wraggy wanted it. He wanted to make Wes sweat.

One day after school I walked home alone. Josh had basketball practice and I had no other friends. People were keeping clear of me. Wes had spread the word that I was trouble.

My school bag was heavy with files and my feet dragged on the pavement as I walked from the high street towards the square. In front of me some younger girls were laughing and squawking like parrots. I felt so lonely that I envied them. Envied the ease with which they linked arms, made loud comments and pushed each other into the gutter.

I needed a friend, somebody to talk to. In the past there'd always been Mum or Gran, but this was something deeper and more dangerous than anything I'd had to cope with before. Imagine Mum's reaction if I told her that I knew who stabbed Andy Wragg, that I'd seen Wes holding a bloodstained knife and yet I'd said nothing to the police. In fact, the afternoon the police were in school I'd played truant. She'd be scandalized. There was no way she could possibly envisage what I was mixed up in and if she knew, she'd march me straight down to the police station then never let me out of the house again.

Crossing the square, my eyes were drawn towards Nazim's shop doorway – the spot where Andy Wragg was found. He'd crawled there, injured and bleeding, moaning with pain. I should have gone back to help him, I shouldn't have run like a coward. I shook my head as I remembered the sounds that had come to me through the darkness. I looked down, tears pricking at my eyes. When I blinked and looked up, I saw Miranda. Her hair was a strange colour, a sort of pinky red, and she seemed to be waiting for somebody.

We hadn't spoken recently. I felt angry that she'd betrayed me, spreading gossip and lies, and was glad she'd kept away from me. I hesitated for a moment, then marched past her, head in the air.

It wasn't until I'd gone past that I remembered I'd promised to buy milk on the way home. So I had to double back and march past Miranda again, trying to avoid her eyes. When I came out of the shop I saw who she'd been waiting for. Leaning against the bars of the shop window, she was deep in conversation with Charlene Wragg. Charlene had her back to me and I hoped I'd be able to scoot past without her seeing me. But just as I was hurrying away, a voice shouted loudly, "Hey Goldie."

It was useless to pretend I hadn't heard.

I turned and waited as they came over; Miranda looked small and pale beside the heavy bulk of Charlene. They were arm in arm, and I could only guess why they were suddenly friends.

Charlene stopped and smiled at me. I was immediately on my guard, but she seemed relaxed and pulled two tickets from her pocket. "Miranda just give me these tickets for your gig. Hope it's worth comin' to."

I didn't reply but stared at Miranda, who at least had the grace to look embarrassed.

"Like her hair?" Charlene asked, grinning. "I done it for 'er."

"It's different," I said.

"Yeah . . . different," Charlene repeated, her cheeks shining like big, pink apples.

For a moment there was silence. Then she cocked her head to one side and the shine on her cheeks turned to a gleam of malice.

"I got a message for yer . . . from my brother."

My heart started to thump and my mouth dried.

"He knows you protectin' Wes Mabbott. But he don't care, he just wants you to stay out of it. Andy wants to sort this 'imself."

I stared blankly at her big balloon face. Thick fog blared through my brain and all I could see were Charlene's pale blue eyes flashing like police sirens.

"You don't get it, do you?" she asked finally.

I shook my head. She looked at me like I was the biggest idiot in creation.

"Andy wants his revenge. 'E'll be back on the streets soon. So you and Mabbott better watch out."

I was aware of Miranda's face looming and bobbing beside Charlene's. "They've set up a straightener," she said.

I must have looked blanker than ever because Charlene explained. "That's the way we do things 'ere. We don't run to the cops, we sort it ourselves. All fair and square," she said. "Andy's just waiting for the right time. Then 'e'll do Wes. An' if you blab to the police, he'll do you too."

I stared at them both, then fixed my eyes on Miranda. I focused on her until she blushed as red as her new hair colour. I wanted to hit her. I wanted to bash her head in until she understood how difficult she'd made things for me. She could have been a friend, she could have tried to understand. But no, she'd joined forces with Charlene. I knew whose side she was on now.

I walked away with my mind churning round and round, thoughts whirling through my brain. What a mess. Some people wanted me to speak up and others wanted me to shut up. I couldn't win. And why was I bothered anyway? What did it matter? They were all as bad as each other. Wes, Andy Wragg, Ralph, Charlene. Let them destroy each other. Why should I risk my neck going to the police? Josh was right. The one positive thing I had was music. The concert had to be a big success and then I'd sing my way out of this godforsaken place.

I was so lost in thought that I walked off the path and almost fell headlong over a bicycle. Luckily a woman shouted just in time and I stopped. I noticed a collection of small bikes abandoned on the grass and through the bushes I could see a group of kids. I wondered what they were up to and peered through the leaves.

There were seven or eight boys clustered together and in their midst stood Wes Mabbott. He was holding out his hand and the kids were dropping money into it. Wes was nodding and smiling, sunlight glancing off his broad forehead, his earring glinting. As other kids came forward he collected more money and I noticed the flash of a heavy gold bracelet on his wrist.

He reached into his pocket and pulled out a small package. Carefully he unwrapped it and doled out tiny pieces. I couldn't see what they were but the kids reached for them eagerly, stowing them deep in their pockets.

When he'd finished he pretended to fake fight with a small boy in a red T-shirt. My skin crawled as I heard him laugh. I watched as he chased the boy, pretending to hit him. And suddenly I knew. He was acting like his usual arrogant self. Within sight of the footpath, he'd been dealing, selling the kids something that I was certain wasn't sweets. He had a carefree, casual air about him. He didn't look like somebody who was worried about anything. He had all the confidence in the world. And I knew as surely as if he'd told me, he'd got his knife back. He wasn't afraid any longer.

CHAPTER SIXTEEN

Sun was filtering through the gaps in my makeshift curtains, dappling the walls and the floor. I rolled over, hot and sweaty, my head still full of lurid dreams. The silence of the house rang in my ears, then a confusion of thoughts crowded in.

I thumped the pillow, closed my eyes and tried to get back to sleep. But the inside of my head was like a torture chamber, sharp voices and disjointed pictures prodding me awake.

I squeezed my eyes shut and tried to blot out my worries, but it was no use. I was haunted. I heard Wes's cackling laugh, heard him saying again and again, "I've got the knife. I've got the knife."

I couldn't get back to sleep and finally I gave up, threw off the covers and padded over to the window. Opening it wide, I stuck out my head and breathed in cool air. Glimmers of pink and orange suffused the sky; it was going to be a beautiful spring day.

Resting my elbows on the sill, I looked towards the bridge. Nobody was about; just a lone dog peeing up against the base of the almond tree. The pink blossom had long gone, and now it was Mum and Nancy's gardens that provided some bright colour. They'd worked hard all spring, planting every container they could find. But when I looked down, I gasped in horror. Something had happened, something dreadful. Petals, stems, leaves and soil lay scattered across the yard – Mum's garden was wrecked.

I gazed open-mouthed. Smashed pots, torn branches and broken canes were spread over the yard. Mum's treasured camellia lay on its side. The gate hung off its hinges and grow bags, emptied of their contents, flapped like crow's wings.

Grabbing my dressing-gown I dashed downstairs and out the front door with some mad hope of minimizing the damage before Mum saw it. Tears blurred my vision as I ran about picking up plants and shrubs. I snatched up some delicate pink and white flowers, their stems tangled, the roots already dry. Then, snatching up an empty container, I pushed the plants down, shovelled in soil and tried to firm the stems upright. Petals drooped over the sides but the effect wasn't too bad – with a bit of luck they might survive.

I scurried back into the kitchen to find a sweeping brush. Mum would be awake soon, I had to sort things out. I swiped at the scattered soil, as anger boiled inside me. I wanted to know who was responsible. Was it Wraggy's lot or Wes?

I didn't have to wait long for an answer. I'd just swept some leaves into a corner, when I turned round to see a big blue circle painted on bricks beside the front door. Inside the circle was a bright blue jagged M, like the devil's fork. M for Mabbott, M for mean, M for maniac. Under cover of darkness, Wes had come up to our house and etched his mark. A warning. *I know where you live. Keep quiet or I'll be back.*

I stormed round the yard in disgust, kicking at broken pottery and throwing flowers into a heap. I felt sick and nervous. I was swallowing great mouthfuls of saliva and my insides were churning like a washing machine.

Banging my way into the kitchen, I fetched a bucket of hot water and some cleaner, then I stood outside in front of the sign and rolled up the sleeves of my dressing-gown. I was determined to scrub out that stupid, rotten symbol if it took me all morning.

I was still scrubbing furiously at the paint when Mum and Dad appeared. Dad went mad, raging round the yard and cursing the vandals. He was all for rushing off and phoning the police. I had a few heart-thumping minutes weighing up the consequences of that action, but before I could say anything Mum talked him out of it.

"What the police gonna do?" she asked. "They got serious crime to deal with. They ain't gonna be interested in a few broken plants."

"But Yvette, you've worked so hard," Dad protested.

Mum didn't reply. She just stood looking down at the broken plant in her hand, tears brimming in her eyes.

I put down my brush, rushed forward and threw my arms round her.

"I'm so sorry, Mum," I said.

She shook her head. "It's not your fault."

Tears ran down my cheeks, spilling on to her hair. Quickly, I kissed her cheek then fled before I gave everything away. Not my fault? Yes it was. It was all my fault. Wes Mabbott had wrecked the yard because he wanted to frighten me. Make sure I wouldn't squeal to the police. He wasn't afraid of me any more because he knew I'd lied. He knew I didn't have the knife.

Upstairs in my room, I buried my head in my arms and cried. I hated myself for being so arrogant. I'd thought I was such a big shot trying to outwit Mabbott, but if I hadn't tried to be clever then Mum's garden would still be intact.

A sense of hopelessness washed over me. I buried my head in the eiderdown and inhaled the sweet musty smell. Instantly I was reminded of Gran.

"Do the right thing, Goldie," I heard her say. But what was right? I hardly knew any more, everything had become so complicated.

Ideas swirled through my brain until I was sick of Wes and knives and blades and imagined interviews in police stations. I rolled on to my back and stared at the ceiling. I should be downstairs helping to clear up, I should be talking to Mum and Dad, I should be . . . happy. Wes Mabbott was destroying my life. Until I'd got this sorted I didn't have a chance.

My mind cleared. I had two choices, either give in to Wes and put myself in his power, or use the evidence I had to defeat him. I decided I'd tell the police what I'd seen, ask for their protection and then it would all be over.

By the time I was dressed my mind was made up and I felt better. I'd tell Mum and Dad everything, get their support and then we'd go to the police. Wes Mabbott had to be stopped.

I pulled on my blazer and raced downstairs but was met halfway by Patrick.

"Don't go down there, Mum's being sick," he said. "Yuck."

I edged past him and sure enough, Dad was holding on to Mum whilst she heaved into the kitchen sink.

I stood for a moment, clutching my stomach, trying to stop myself heaving in sympathy.

Dad turned his head. "Pass us a glass, Goldie. Your mum needs some water."

I opened the cupboard and gave him a tumbler. Mum's hand was shaking as she drank. She looked terrible.

"I'll stay home. Look after Mum," I offered.

Dad shook his head. "No. It's all right. Nancy'll be round in a minute. She'll keep your Mum company."

"But, Dad I..."

"Goldie, don't bother me. You can see your Mum's in a state."

I backed off but I didn't want to leave. I hung around in the doorway waiting for Mum to feel better. I had to tell them. But suddenly Dad turned round and his eyes flashed angrily.

"Goldie, you'll be late for school."

I stepped forward. "Let me look after Mum, I don't mind. Dad, please."

I waited for an answer but Mum swayed and vomited into the sink again. Dad rubbed her back, murmuring softly. I stood wondering what to do when suddenly Dad turned, shot me a furious look and rapped out one word, "Go".

My shoulders slumped as I picked up my heavy bag. I had no option but to obey. When Dad made his mind up about something, that was it. My confession would have to wait.

Walking towards the bridge, I saw a figure lolling against one of the pillars. I almost ran back when I saw who it was. Couldn't I get any peace? I gripped the strap of my heavy bag, gritted my teeth and prepared to walk past.

It was Ralph, waiting silent and still until I was level with him. He made a tutting, disapproving noise with his tongue as I walked past, my head in the air, trying to look as if I hadn't noticed him.

Just after I'd passed him he shouted, "Get the message, did ya?"

I swallowed hard. I knew which message – Mum's

wrecked plants. But I didn't want him to see how upset I was, so I squared my shoulders and carried on walking. I was seething with hate but I told myself that before the day ended, I'd have my revenge.

I heard his footsteps behind me but I was determined not to look back, not to betray the slightest hint of fear. Then I saw Wes standing just the other side of the bridge.

I veered away from him but he moved fast, coming up beside me and whispering urgently. "You lied to me, Goldie Moon. Told me you had somethin' of mine. But you didn't, did ya?"

I kept on walking and said nothing. But Wes wasn't easily put off.

"See, somebody was kind enough to give it back to me," he carried on. "Seems you didn't have it at all. You just thought you'd worry me and maybe buy yourself some protection. Well, you ain't so clever now your garden's busted, eh? And let me tell you, if you have any thoughts 'bout going to the police, I'll do more than wreck your garden. I make sure your house burn."

Somehow I kept walking; somehow I kept my cool, but I was jelly inside. He stood in front of me, his eyes blazing.

"If you know what's good for you," he snarled, "You and your family will go back to where you come from."

I gave him a cold, hard stare then I walked on. I wouldn't listen to him. I wasn't going to be intimidated. My family wouldn't be leaving. We were staying put and I'd show him.

I was going to do the concert. The band would be a big success and everybody would love us. *Eat your heart out, Wes Mabbott. We – me and the band – are going places you can only dream of.*

CHAPTER SEVENTEEN

Over the next few weeks I concentrated on preparing for the gig, throwing myself into rehearsals like they were my salvation.

The band worked really hard, rehearsing three or four times a week. It took a lot of energy, but I loved it. I enjoyed performing and my voice was getting stronger and more versatile. I worked on phrasing, adding real character to the lyrics and I discovered a gritty, gutsy way of singing that added a raw edge to our songs.

On stage I was developing my own style of dancing and moving; it wasn't an act any more, it had become part of me, part of my music. And as we rehearsed, the band got better and better. Tickets for the gig were selling well. We received lots of support from family and friends and, let's face it, there wasn't much competition – the estate was hardly a regular venue for rock concerts.

On Friday, the night of our final rehearsal, I walked home from school alone. Josh was at a basketball game so I dawdled along by myself, singing softly. Ahead of me were groups of pupils strolling towards the estate. I lagged behind, noticing Ralph amongst them. I didn't want to bump into him or any of his undesirable friends.

By the time I reached the square the groups had split up, scattering in different directions. I walked towards the shops humming one of Josh's tunes. It was a warm day, the steel grille on the bookies glinted in the afternoon sun and heat rose from the pavements. Two little girls in bright dresses squealed as they chased each other, a dog bouncing and yapping at their side.

I spotted Ralph with two other lads sitting on one of the benches, school shirts unbuttoned, sleeves rolled up. They were handing round cigarettes. As I walked towards them they lit up.

"Hey, Goldie, sing a song for us," Ralph shouted.

His mates laughed.

"Your gig tomorrow night, ain't it?" he asked.

I kept on walking.

"Seen the posters?" another lad shouted. "Fascist bastards!"

I was striding away from them but my step faltered. What did he mean? I half-turned, hesitating.

Ralph stood up and flexed his arms. "They need sortin'," he said. "We'll kick their white asses, yeh?"

His mates laughed again, but I went cold inside.

When I drew level with the Community Centre, I saw what they meant. Zoë was running a great publicity campaign, posters for the concert were everywhere. But the ones here were defaced – giant red swastikas daubed all over them.

I stared in disgust. Why couldn't they leave us alone? All we wanted to do was sing and play and give people a great night out. Was it asking too much for something good to happen in this cursed place?

I wanted to tear all the posters down. What use were they now? As I stood there, biting back angry tears, Zoë came out of the Centre.

"Good job I've got spares," she said, nodding towards the hoardings. "They're off their heads, that lot. Don't know which is worse. Mabbott's gang, taggin' everywhere with their stupid blue circles, or Wraggy's lot with their friggin' swastikas. Not much to choose between 'em."

She put down the new posters and a pot of glue and wrapped an arm round my shoulders. "Don't worry. Nobody's gonna ruin the concert. I'll make sure of that. No troublemakers welcome."

"Thanks, Zoë," I sniffed.

She patted my shoulder, then pulled a brush from her shirt pocket and set to work.

"Why do they do it?" I moaned.

"No brains, no hope," Zoë answered, smoothing down a poster.

"I'll give you a hand," I said, putting down my school bag.

"No. You go home. Get yourself organized. I'm comin' to the rehearsal tonight so you'd better be on crackin' form. And. . ." She smiled, "I've got a surprise. A certain special somebody is coming to the gig tomorrow. A well-connected record producer who is very interested in your band. Said he'd pop in an' have a listen."

She stared at me, blinking her big grey eyes, waiting for my reaction.

When the news sank in, excitement fizzed through me. I spluttered and grinned, then felt as if I'd swallowed a box of fireworks. A record producer! That could mean recording deals, fame, fortune, TV!

"Go on," Zoë said. "Go an' get ready. Opportunity knocks!"

I didn't need telling twice. "Thanks, Zoë," I shrieked, throwing my arms round her and giving her a hug before picking up my bag and rushing off home.

I practically skipped all the way to the bridge, celebrating as I walked. A record producer. I hardly dared think about it in case it didn't happen – but it might, it might! Tomorrow night could be the most important night of my life.

When I reached the bridge I was reminded all too forcibly of who could ruin it. Giant red swastikas and letter Ws daubed the pillars, obliterating some of the blue Mabbott symbols. Tension crackled in the air – sizzling over the empty space, whirling under the bridge, bouncing off the concrete. Behind me, sunlit windows winked like spotlights.

In the glaring sunshine our little yard looked stripped and bare. Nancy had given Mum some of her plants but it wasn't as colourful and abundant as before; the life had gone out of it and so had Mum's enthusiasm. I closed the gate, opened the front door as quietly as I could and climbed softly up to my room. I needed time to think.

Unloading my heavy bag on to the bed I went over to the window and picked up a pale creamy shell. My fingers smoothed the pearly spirals. I put it to my ear and heard the crash of waves. My mind was a tangle of thoughts. I didn't know what to do. Tomorrow was our big chance but if the gangs staged a fight, it would be a disaster.

I put the shell down and looked at the photo of Gran. "Give me strength," I begged.

She looked back at me. "Courage, Goldie," I heard her say. And I knew what I must do. Face the enemy.

It wasn't difficult to find Wes. He was on one of the benches in the square – the same place I'd seen Ralph and company earlier. Two little kids were sitting with him, cadging a drag of his cigarette.

He didn't move as I approached but I knew he'd seen me. I went closer, until I stood right in front of him.

"Can I talk to you?" I asked.

He leant forward, sucking on his cigarette and blowing smoke over my shirt front.

"Always a pleasure," he said chuckling softly.

He looked up at me, his narrow eyes squinting.

"Wes," I said softly. "The posters. All the graffiti. What's going on?"

He snapped his fingers and the two little kids scarpered. I sat down on the end of the bench and felt his eyes on me.

"It's Wraggy," he said. "He's out for my blood."

"Can't you stop him?" I asked.

He threw down his cigarette and ground it under his heel.

"Wish I could. I'm not too eager to get a knife in my ribs."

I winced at his words. "You won't fight at the concert, will you? Please, Wes. Loads of people are coming – families, little kids, old people."

He turned away and spat on the ground. "What ya doin' this for anyway? I tol' you. I don't want you in no band – white bitch."

"I don't want anybody to get hurt," I persisted.

He slid across the bench until his leg was touching mine. I hardly dared breathe; my heart quickened, thumping loudly.

Suddenly, he thrust out a hand and grasped my shirt sleeve. His hand slipped round my shoulder and gripped the top of my arm. He leant so close that I was choked by stale, smoky breath.

"Tell you what," he said, his voice soft and purry. "If you do somethin' for me, I guarantee, there be no fightin' at the gig tomorrow night. Know what I'm sayin'?"

His hand pulled at the hem of my shirt. A kind of numb, swirling panic took hold of me. I closed my eyes. His chin scratched against my cheek, his lips were close to my mouth. It's just a kiss – it doesn't matter, I thought. And I had some mad idea that perhaps I could persuade him not to fight if I let him kiss me. But he was leaning over me, pressing up against me and I felt a surge of sickness rising in my stomach. His hand grasped at my shoulder, slid down over my breast. I tensed.

Wes gripped my chin. "What's wrong? You know you want it. You been wantin' it ever since you first saw me. That's why you come here."

"Yes, all right." I said.

He held on to me tightly, squeezing my chin so that it hurt.

"You wouldn't bullshit me, would you?" His laugh was brittle as ice.

"No," I said. "I . . . look . . . if there's no trouble at the concert, I could meet you afterwards."

He laughed again, a muffled, unsettling chortle, like a gremlin gone mad. "What's lover boy gonna say to that?"

I grasped his hand and squeezed it tight. "I don't care about Josh no more," I said. "It's you I want. But you've got to stop the fight."

"I don't know if I can stop it."

"Wes, you the big shot round 'ere," I said softly. "Everybody do what you say. If you tell the brothers not to fight, then they won't. You the one everybody listens to. If you give your word, I'll know the gig is safe."

He smiled, his gold tooth glinting. "I'll see what I can do."

Hope rushed through me. "Great," I said. "You promise?"

I shouldn't have pushed it. Quick as a cornered rat he grabbed my arm and held it tight. "You one cool bitch," he said. "You better keep that promise, right? You see me after the gig and we gonna be real friendly."

He pulled me roughly into his arms and started kissing me. Hot, rasping kisses over my face and hair. Then he was holding me tight and sucking at my neck.

"No," I said, pulling away and squirming under his arm. "Wait till tomorrow. I've got to go now."

When I reached home, I sped up to the bathroom and splashed cold water over my face and into my mouth, washing away Wes's touch. Then, I went into my room and sat on the edge of the bed. I felt weak and trembly, as if I'd had a big shock. But I was glowing with triumph too. I'd made a dangerous bargain but hopefully it would work. Wes wouldn't fight. We'd play a brilliant gig and then all I had to do was figure out how to avoid his advances later.

A soft knock sounded and the door opened. It was Mum.

"Are you all right?" she asked.

"Yes, I'm fine."

She stepped into the room. "What you doin' creepin' in and out the house?"

"Sorry."

"What's wrong?"

"Nothing."

She came over to me.

"I'm just a bit tired," I said

I could feel Mum's eyes on me.

"You not been yourself lately. You seem distracted – thinkin', dreamin', worryin'. I see you. What the matter, girl? Aren't you lookin' forward to the gig?"

She sat beside me and removed the sweatshirt I'd flung over my knees.

I smoothed the hair back from my face and smiled. "Yes, I'm looking forward to it. I'm just a bit worried about tonight. It's our last rehearsal so everything's got to be spot on."

Mum smiled. "Course it will be. You been practisin' so hard."

"I know. But it's a lot of pressure."

"You never bothered about pressure before, girl. You'd live on the stage if you could. So what different now?"

"I don't know."

"You don't know, or you ain't tellin'," Mum said firmly. She was staring at me. "There's some trouble in the air, am I right? All these symbols scrawled on pillar and post. That boy gettin' stabbed. You not mixed up in anything are ya?"

"Oh Mum, course I'm not."

"No, you have more sense than get involved in anything so pointless, I know that. These gang boys they got nothin' better to do than be causin' trouble. They got no values. No pride." She pushed a wayward strand of hair back from my face and stroked my neck. "You better than that, Goldie. You got ambition. You got a long ways to go."

I closed my eyes and relaxed as she massaged my neck and shoulders. It would be so easy to tell all my troubles – to lay my burden down. But I couldn't. It was too late. Tomorrow was the gig. I had to think positive. I mustn't let anything stand in its way.

I sat still and silent as her hands moved over my skin, glad of her warmth, happy to feel loved and supported. Then, she tapped my chin and turned my face toward her.

"You enjoy yourself tomorrow night, you hear?" she said.

I put my head on her arm. "Yes, course I will," I promised.

"How's it going with Josh?" she asked.

I grinned. "Great. He's the best part of everything."

"He a good boy. Me and your Dad, we like him."

"I'm glad."

"You not worried about nothin' with Josh? He not pushin' you?"

I glanced sideways and Mum's face was a picture of sympathy. Her "you can tell me anything and everything" look. But much as would have loved a cosy talk about Josh, it wasn't the right moment.

"No worries about Josh, Mum, honest."

Mum patted my shoulder. "Well, if you sure. My heart always open, you know that." She ran her hand up and down my arm, massaging, soothing. "Problems is all impossible until they solved. You know that, Goldie?"

I nodded and took her hand, glad of its warmth, glad she was with me. "Yes Mum, I know."

She squeezed my hand, then let go and stood up. "By the way, you figured out what you gonna wear tomorrow night?"

"No."

She threw up her hands, pretending shock and horror. "A stage appearance and Goldie Moon got nothin' to wear. She must be preoccupied!"

"I'll find something."

Mum shook her head. "You a puzzle, girl." She walked towards the door. "Well, I'm goin' to see to dinner. You better get yourself ready."

When she'd gone I flopped back on the bed and thumped my old eiderdown.

"Don't worry, Mum. I won't let them win," I said out loud. "Tomorrow night I'm going to get up on that stage and I'm going to sing."

CHAPTER EIGHTEEN

As I walked towards the Centre I was full of nervous excitement. I tried to ignore the catcalls from a gang of youths, the broken glass and litter and the swastikas creeping like poisonous spiders over the walls. Think positive, I kept saying to myself, and to help me, I sang one of Josh's songs:

"You live in amongst the garbage and shit
You called out to fight, you called hypocrite
But you gotta keep on, ain't no alternative
Tell it like it is. Be positive."

A battle cry for unsung heroes, Josh called it. "Ain't hard to be different," he'd told me. "But it's real tough to be the same. Same as everybody else who do some crappy job every day and get just enough pay to keep body and soul together. They ain't never gonna be rich but they keep on goin'."

At first, I'd thought he was joking, but I could see by his face that he meant it. I understood the sentiment but it didn't shake my resolve. I wanted to be different, I wanted to be a star. Mum was right – the gang warfare was because the kids were bored, they had no self-worth. Well, I knew I was worth something and I was going to prove it. Now I'd fixed Wes nothing would stop me.

By the time I arrived at the Centre I was raring to go. I looked at the clean, bright posters – no new graffiti, thank goodness. The band's name was up there in big bold letters, and I felt a thrill of pride.

Well, no turning back now. It was our final rehearsal. I squared my shoulders. "Shine on, Goldie Moon, you can do it, the band's good. Be bold, be confident, no fear." And with my head held high, I walked through the foyer and into the empty, echoing hall.

Tiger was setting up the amps and cursing our primitive equipment. He stomped back and forth as Josh sat on the edge of the stage tuning his guitar. When he saw me, he smiled.

"You OK?"

"Yeah. I'm fine."

"You look good."

I smiled. "I know."

"We gonna get this show on the road or what?" Tiger interrupted, glaring at us across his keyboard.

Josh nudged me, rolled his eyes and whispered, "Better get rockin' – the Tiger is roarin'." Then he put down his guitar, flexed his hands into claws and roared.

I giggled but cast an anxious glance in Tiger's direction. One day Josh would go too far. Luckily, Tiger was absorbed in taping down some wires and hadn't noticed Josh's antics – anyway, he was too busy moaning.

"Who put this amp here? Christ, this equipment's shit.

We need a proper mixing desk. The acoustics in here are crap. What can you expect with all this stuff around? It deadens everything." He gestured wildly towards a folded trampoline, crash mats and badminton nets.

"This ceiling's too low. Listen." He played a thin reedy chord. "Sounds like a damp fart in a high wind."

Nazim, who'd just finished setting up his drums, gave a loud thump on the bass drum followed by a resounding roll. Tiger raised his head and glared. By the time we'd set up, his mood was as spiky as his hair; bad vibes screeched like feedback.

Thankfully, the first two numbers went well and I was just beginning to relax when, on the third song, I messed up.

"Shit, Goldie, where were you?" Tiger boomed.

I coughed nervously. "It sounded different," I said.

"Well it ain't. It's just the same goddamn intro we've played every bleedin' time, right?"

"OK," I murmured.

"We're doing this gig tomorrow night. You only get one chance to cut it," Tiger snapped.

Then he turned to Nazim and blasted him for what he called "fancy drumming".

"Just keep the friggin' beat, man," Tiger warned.

My confidence was oozing away; my eyes welled with tears. We had to get everything right tonight, but the song was ragged, we were all over the place; even Josh wasn't playing with his usual commitment.

Thankfully, we managed to get ourselves together and did a couple more numbers reasonably well, but Tiger was anxious, pushing to go right through the set list. Tension grew: Josh wanted to do one of his songs unplugged; Tiger wanted to do it the way he'd arranged it. Josh refused.

"I want it simple. All them backing sounds, you can't hear the words. Words is what I wrote, man. I want people to hear 'em." His voice had a hard edge. "You accuse Nazim of doing fancy drummin' and then you want to do a fancy number on my song. It's a simple song, man, not a damn space odyssey."

I felt tired and drained. I needed a break and risked speaking up.

"Look, I think we've done enough. I'm sure we'll be fine tomorrow. When it's the real thing you have to be sharp, you get this adrenalin rush and. . ."

I looked across at Tiger, expecting some sarcastic put-down, but he just averted his head, cracking his knuckles in irritation.

I continued. "If we mess up on something, so what? It's not going to be, like, a total disaster. People know it's our first gig."

Of course, Tiger bristled at that. Running his fingers through his stiff blond hair he sighed heavily. I thought he was going to blow up, but he just bowed his head and muttered into his keyboard. Even so, I was glad that Josh came to stand beside me.

"She right, man," he said. "We done enough. You forgettin' that we doin' this for enjoyment. You getting too tense. Let things be, now. My reputation riding on this and I know what we done is cool. We tight, we sharp, we polished, better than any local band I ever 'eard."

Tiger looked at Nazim. "What do you reckon, Naz? You ain't satisfied with this shit, eh?"

Nazim shrugged. "If we start changing things now, it'll throw us. We could go on for ever – nothin's ever perfect, is it?"

And with that he stood up and reached for his jacket. "Don't know about you, but I got things to do. I'm off."

"Hold on, mate," Tiger shouted. "At least let's change the running order."

But Nazim took no notice of him and began to pack away.

Tiger glared and punched a couple of keys. "Amateurs . . . amateurs," he muttered.

Josh nodded. "If you say so."

As I started to unscrew the mike stand, a door banged and I looked up to see Zoë, waving her arms and looking as excited as Christmas.

"Don't go yet, Naz," she said, catching hold of him. "Listen. I've fixed it."

She flew up to the stage. A tall, skinny figure in a ribbed T-shirt and black leather trousers, like a long stick of liquorice, her red hair sticking up like she'd stuck her finger in an electric socket.

Nazim followed her. "Fixed what?" he asked.

She bounded on to the stage. "The man I know, the record producer. He's coming."

She looked at each of us in turn, grinning from ear to ear. Then she turned to me. "Goldie, didn't you tell 'em?" she asked in an astonished voice.

"No," I confessed. "I was going to but. . ."

"Spit it out, then," Tiger said impatiently.

Zoë was jigging about, hardly able to contain herself. "I told Goldie. This friend said he'd come and have a listen. I knew he was in the recording business, thought he was a producer or something. Anyway, he's just been on the phone and it turns out he's only the friggin' A & R guy from Margin records."

Our mouths hung open as she rushed over to Josh and hugged him, then she started waving her arms. "The friggin' A & R guy, for Margin records. The man in charge of scouting for new talent. And he's coming to the gig."

Nobody spoke for a moment. Our eyes were glazed, our bottom lips hit the floor. I was stunned. I stopped breathing for minutes then I breathed in, filled up with air, rose off the ground and floated in mid-air.

"Isn't it brilliant?" Zoë asked.

"Oh, yes," I said from my lofty height, somewhere between the spotlights. . .

"Wicked," Josh said.

"Fantastic," Nazim added.

And then I came down from the ceiling and everybody was laughing and hugging, except Tiger, who was standing, looking dead white and nervous.

"Come on, Tiger, you look like somebody's just eaten your winning lottery ticket," Zoë cried.

"Oh, Tiger," I pleaded. "Be happy, this is brilliant news."

"Just 'ope he's not some poncy git," Tiger growled.

I took his hand. "Don't worry. It'll be fine. I know it," I said.

"We're not ready," Tiger said tightly. "We're not prepared."

"It's our chance, Tiger. Our big chance," I said, squeezing his hand. "I know we can do it."

"Margin records," Nazim said. "Whoa. They're big."

"Too big," Tiger moaned.

Zoë made a wry face at him. "You be nice to the man, Tiger. If he signs you up, you'll be made. No more crap equipment. You'll be able to afford the best goddamned friggin' state-of-the-art techno wizardry you've ever dreamt of. You'll have software comin' out your ears."

She caught my hand and raised it in the air. "It's number one. It's *Top of the Pops*. It's No Fear."

Tiger shrugged and walked away, but he couldn't dampen our spirits. As we packed away we were grinning at each other and buzzing with the news.

When all the gear was stowed in the office I stood on the lip of the stage, looking out over the empty hall and trying to psych myself up for tomorrow night's performance. It was amazing. I could hardly believe it. Our first gig and this record-company guy was coming. I prayed I wouldn't mess up, that everything would go great, that nobody would spoil it.

I walked over to Zoë and spoke quietly to her. "Zoë. Tomorrow night – you won't let Wes Mabbott or Andy Wragg in, will you?"

She raised her eyebrows and snorted. "What do ya think I am? Mad? No chance. I've got some heavies on the door. Harder to get past them than a rampagin' rhino."

She put an arm round my neck. "Look, don't sweat. I've got everything organized. All you've got to do is sing, Goldie Moon. Sing like a star."

I tried to smile but a sudden shudder went through me. Would Wes keep away? If he did, how was I to avoid him afterwards? Was I crazy, or what?

Zoë picked up on my mood. "You're tired. Go home and get some rest. I'll open up about six-thirty tomorrow . . . and. . ." she danced a daft jig, "I'll be ready to party."

Josh laughed. "Can't wait," he said. He put his arm round my shoulder as we said goodbye and we walked out into the damp night of the square. He hummed one of his tunes as we walked but I couldn't relax; my stomach was tightening into knots. I felt like a traitor.

An old woman with a shopping trolley crossed in front of us, and some kids were racing round on roller blades. It seemed odd for people to be going about their everyday business when I was entangled in a web of excitement and terror. Tomorrow could be the best or worst day of my life.

Whatever happened, I hoped we'd play a stormer. A few times in rehearsals it had happened. Josh improvising great stuff on guitar, Tiger instinctively playing along; real telepathy between them, and then we'd all be winging it, playing and singing together, a kind of unspoken magic entering our souls. We'd take off and fly.

I was praying everything would be all right as Josh squeezed my arm, cutting into my thoughts. "My Dad's coming to the gig. He wants to meet you."

I was so startled that for a moment I could only mumble, "Oh . . . er . . . good."

I'd never met Josh's dad. There were times when I almost felt he didn't exist or that Josh just used him as an excuse.

Whenever we needed somewhere to go, he never suggested his place. He'd say, "Oh, Dad will be sleeping" or "Dad's about to come home from work" or "Dad'll want to eat." Sometimes, I thought perhaps it was because the flat was untidy or dirty or something. I mean, two men living together, maybe they didn't clean up much.

When I got over the surprise, I said I'd be really glad to meet his dad at last.

"I haven't been hiding 'im, he been doing a lot of overtime lately. We savin' so we can get a new place. It so damp in our flat – walls and windows runnin' with condensation and cockroaches crawlin' everywhere. Council supposed to be pullin' all the blocks down and rehousin' us but that was two years ago."

We stopped at the battered, cracked glass doors to Josh's block.

"I want to meet your dad. See what wonderful man made you," I said.

Josh laughed. He was uncomfortable when I went all serious on him. "You're sure you don't want me to walk you home? he said.

"No, I'll be all right," I answered. There was no way I wanted us to bump into Wes.

CHAPTER NINETEEN

Saturday morning, I staggered downstairs into the kitchen.

"Hey watcha! 'Ere she is, Miss Celebrity. Tonight's the big night, eh? Fame and fortune awaits!" Nancy trilled, giving me a big, beaming smile. She was spooning seedlings into plastic trays and emphasizing her words with a wave of the trowel, leaving a fine trail of soil on the floor and worktop.

Mum reached for a cloth to mop up. "Good mornin', Golden Child. How you feelin'? Ready for the big night?" she asked.

"Couldn't be better," I answered.

She turned to look at me.

"No, really, how you feelin'?"

I pretended to test the temperature of my neck and forehead. "Hot. Hot as a chilli pepper and rarin' to go," I said.

"That's my girl," Mum smiled. "All the folk from Blackheath comin'. Carlo, Chola, Gemma, her mum, Marlon, Mrs Winter and half the choir."

"Brilliant!" I said.

Then came the first shudder of panic. Everybody was up and dressed and busy and there was no sign of breakfast on the table. "What time is it?" I asked.

"Ten-thirty," Mum answered. "We let you lie in. Figured you needed your beauty sleep."

Now my temperature really did rocket. I scratched around the kitchen like a dog with fleas. How had it happened? How could I have slept so late?

"Oh no, I'll never be ready on time," I moaned.

Mum grabbed my shoulders. "Stand still, girl. There's eight hours to go yet. You got plenty a time."

"Mum," I protested. "You know it takes ages to do my hair and my nails and..."

"Yeah, an' you gotta clean your room an' cook us some dinner an' help with these plants an'...."

I was so panicky that for a moment I thought she was serious.

"Oh, Mum, I..."

She tugged playfully at my hair and laughed. "I'm jus' sassin' you. This your day, girl. You think I gonna bother you with chores today? But one thing. Before you start preenin' and pamperin', you need to eat somethin' nourishin'."

She moved round Nancy to get to the sink and started to wash her hands. I knew she was about to make me one of her huge breakfasts, so I quickly snatched a banana from the fruit bowl and made towards the door. "A banana is nourishing," I said. "Look, a skinful of sunshine."

Mum turned from the sink and looked at me sternly. "You need stamina, girl."

"Stamina and custard?" I asked.

Nancy laughed. "Hope you're playin' some good ole rock 'n' roll tonight," she said. "You 'aven't seen me jive, 'ave ya?"

Flourishing her trowel she danced, jiggling her hips, her elbows out, her shoulders rotating, stirring ripples of flesh.

I pictured the concert: audience politely tapping their feet and clapping, whilst Nancy danced in the aisle, pulsating like a pneumatic drill. I turned away to hide my grin.

"I think things have moved on a bit since rock 'n' roll," Dad said. "They don't dance much nowadays, just twitch like robots."

"That's where you're wrong then, 'cos you can definitely dance to some of our songs," I said, firmly. "And we might throw in a couple of oldies for you and Nancy and the other wrinklies."

Dad laughed. "Right, you're on. You've never seen my Mick Jagger impression have you?"

"Yes, Dad, many times," I said.

Mum came over and rested her chin on top of Dad's head. "Your dad and I so proud of you," she said.

I blushed. "Thanks, Mum."

She patted my arm. "Now you go and get yourself ready. 'Ave a nice relaxing bath. The immersion's been on an hour."

I ran a hot, deep bath and sank down into the oily depths, but I couldn't relax. I kept bobbing in and out, shaving my legs, scrubbing my elbows. When I got out I skidded back to my room and bounced around like a coiled spring. I sorted through make-up, filed my nails, made faces at myself in the mirror, then pulled off my hair band and shook out my hair. *Come on, Goldie. Get a grip on yourself. Tonight's the night. Relax, sister, chill out.*

I chose an old Motown tape and sang along with Gladys Knight while I sorted through my clothes. A sad collection of old jeans, faded T-shirts and one skirt that had wrinkled in the wash. My underwear was even worse. A few pairs of checked knickers, elastic sprouting from the seams, and my bras were a whiter shade of grey. I sighed and threw everything back in the drawer. The grunge look was popular again.

At least I had plenty of make-up, a bag full of unused birthday and Christmas presents. I chose dark red nail varnish, applied it carefully, then danced around waving my nails as I sang.

Mum knocked at the door. "Hey, you should be restin' that voice. I thought you were relaxin'! 'Ere, I brought some milk and a sandwich."

"Thanks, Mum."

I glanced at the tray she'd set down and next to it I saw a package wrapped in dark red tissue paper tied up with a pink bow.

"What's that?" I asked.

"Open it and see."

I pulled at the pink bow and unwrapped the folds of tissue. The afternoon sun caught the rich, deep swathes of material as I lifted up a dress, a dress so beautiful it made me gasp. It was red velvet, the colour of wine, shimmering with crimson light and tiny gold stars. It was dramatic and stylish, yet pretty and delicate – a dream of a dress.

"Oh, Mum, it's beautiful. It must have cost a fortune. Where did you. . .?"

"Don't you worry about that now. Let's just see if it fits."

I didn't need any encouragement. I jumped out of my jeans and slipped the dress over my head. Mum turned me round and zipped it up at the back. I stepped up on to the bed to look in the mirror and I loved what I saw.

"Oh, Mum, it's wonderful. It fits perfectly," I cried.

I bent down to see my face and, against the bold colour of the dress, my eyes blazed and my skin glowed. Straightening up again, I turned sideways and saw how the dress showed off my figure. It clung to my breasts and hips without puckering; caressing my body, showing I was slim, but shapely, and all the while the stars gleamed softly. And it was short, shorter than I thought Mum would permit.

I drew myself up to my full height. "Is it too short?" I asked.

"Well, you gotta show off those great legs of yours when you on stage. Strut your stuff like Tina Turner," Mum laughed. Then she said, "I think maybe you growed a bit. I measured it 'gainst that dress I made you last Christmas."

"Mum, did you make this?" I asked in amazement, running my hands over the smooth velvet.

"Would it make any difference if I said I did?"

"No, I'd love it, whatever. It's gorgeous," I replied. "It's better than any shop dress. It's unique and I love the stars. What made you think to do them?"

"Oh, I don't know, they seemed appropriate. Now come down 'ere before you fall off that bed. I want to see if the hem is level. I might take it down a bit. I only tacked it."

I jumped down. "No, Mum. I like it the way it is," I said, twirling round and making the skirt fly out.

Mum tutted and pretended to disapprove. "Well, you just be careful you don't bend down too much. And stop admiring yourself. You know what your Gran say."

"Yes, I know. Pride come afore a plummet or a prize," I said.

Mum kissed me and smiled. "Oh, you look a picture, honey. You sure do. I tol' Nancy the colour be just right."

I hugged Mum tightly and kissed her. "Mum, you're brilliant. Somehow I feel the gig is going to be just fine now."

"Course it will be fine. Hm. Them stars come out just right with that gold thread. Just right. Take it off now, though, or you'll spoil it."

She turned to go but then stopped, pointing to the bed. "Oh, I nearly forgot. There's something else to open. Nancy's contribution."

A small parcel lay in the middle of my bed. I tore it open

and scooped up a handful of shiny, wine-coloured satin. It separated into bra and shorts – exactly the same colour as my dress.

Mum kissed my forehead. "I better get back to my gardenin' and you better try these new things on."

"Thanks, Mum . . . and thank Nancy," I said.

When she'd gone I went over to the window sill and picked up Gran's photograph. She was smiling serenely. "Make a wish for me, Gran," I murmured. "Wish that it goes great tonight and the A & R man is knocked out by us."

Pulling my dressing-gown tight around me, I crossed to the bed and stroked the rich velvety folds of the dress. The gold stars gleamed, tiny sparks of light twinkling against the old eiderdown. Softly, I began to sing – a spiritual. *"Let me lay my burden down, Lord; Comin' through to joy."*

I sang as I slipped out of my dressing-gown and tried on my new underwear. When I looked at myself in the mirror, I stopped singing and smiled. What would Josh think if he saw me now? I sat down on the bed and drifted into the type of daydream no respectable fifteen-year-old girl should have.

An hour later, I was panicking. I had make-up to do and hadn't finished my hair, which was always tricky. I let it dry naturally because a hair dryer made it frizz; when it was just at the right stage of dampness I had to comb warm oil into it.

I spent ages dividing my hair into sections, combing and smoothing. When I stood in front of the mirror I saw it had all been worth it. My hair hung smooth and silky, falling in a shining curtain around my shoulders.

I wasn't used to applying make-up. Mum and Dad didn't really approve, and to be honest I thought I looked OK without it, but I knew stage lights tended to wash features out and I didn't want to appear ghostly. But neither did I want to plaster it on and look like a tart. Getting the balance right was going to be difficult.

My skin's dark enough not to need foundation, but I put powder on my nose to stop it shining, then brushed sparkly blusher on to my cheek bones. I wanted to make the most of my eyes so I tried outlining the sockets, but I overdid it and ended up looking like some hollow-eyed corpse. I was giggling as I wiped most of it off but luckily when I'd done that, my eyes looked fine, they had a sort of soft, smudgy but quite dramatic look. I added mascara and lipstick and examined my handiwork in the mirror. Not bad at all. I didn't look dramatically different – it was still me – but a bolder, brighter me.

I reached for my dress, slipped it over my head and was just about to find my black platforms when I remembered a pair of red shoes that were in the dressing-up box. They were Mum's, saved from the seventies, an outrageous concoction of red and purple straps with high stacked heels. I found them and put them on.

Pushing back my bed, I manoeuvred so I could see all of myself in the mirror. Yes, a real transformation! Chic and elegant, with a hint of wild rock-chick – just the right image. Or was I kidding myself? No. I posed in front of the mirror, shimmying my hips and pretending to hold the mike, then I pouted my lips and sent myself a kiss. *Goldie, you are one cool babe and now you can prove to the audience – not only is this girl the business, she sure as hell can sing.*

I twirled around making the skirt fly out. Good job Nancy bought the type of satin knickers that looked like shorts!

When I was ready I carefully took off the dress and shoes wrapped them in polythene, put on an old pair of jeans and T-shirt. This was it. No turning back now.

With the send off they gave me you'd have thought I was embarking on a round-the-world trip. Hugs and kisses from Mum and Dad, a thump on the back from Patrick and an armful of cards from friends and people in my old choir back in Blackheath.

"See you backstage afterwards," Mum said.

"Mum, it's the Community Centre, not Wembley Arena."

Dad laughed. "Just make sure you don't fall off the stage in those high heels," he said.

Josh was waiting for me in front of the flats, guitar case in hand, wearing his familiar shorts and T-shirt but, I noted, new red baseball boots and hair freshly waxed. When I reached him he held out his hand.

"Tonight's the night," he said. "You ready?"

I nodded.

"New dress?" he asked, gesturing to the polythene bag draped over my arm.

I nodded.

"You look good," he said.

I smiled and nodded.

"You saving your voice for later?" he asked.

I grinned. "Just nervous," I said.

"You'll be fine," he answered, squeezing my hand.

As we walked down the path to the Centre, I noticed how quiet everything was. Nobody was about and the air seemed heavy and still, like it does before a storm.

"Josh," I said quietly, "Have you noticed anything?"

"What?"

"It's so quiet. There's no kids about."

He looked round.

"Yeah," he said, slowly. "It's strange, kind of unreal."

When we reached the square, everywhere was deserted. No groups of smokers, no skateboarders, no cyclists. No kids kicking Coke cans, just lots of litter and graffiti.

"Look, it's empty," I said.

Josh looked round the square and frowned. "Don't mean nothin'," he said.

"But it's not natural."

"No," he said. Then he smiled. "They're all gettin' ready for the gig."

"I hope so," I said.

Josh put his arm round my shoulders and kissed my cheek. "You nervous, girl, but you know, everything's gonna be jus' fine. I know it."

CHAPTER TWENTY

Inside the hall, Zoë was working the lights. First a soft gold light suffused the stage, then a ghostly blue glow, followed by a surge of red. I pictured myself out there, singing, and my stomach churned.

We checked the sound, Tiger checked the set lists, Zoë checked we all had a bottle of water and a towel was put on Nazim's drum seat. I raised and lowered the mike, Josh pocketed his plectrums and Tiger reminded us of the encore. Then we all had to admit there was nothing else to do but wait for an audience.

"Come on," Zoë instructed. "You can wait in my office till the place fills up then I'll give you the nod when we're ready."

She ushered us into her little room, brought in two more chairs so we could all sit down, then disappeared to do door and ticket duty.

I looked at the others in their old jeans and T-shirts and decided it was time to transform myself.

Luckily there was hardly anybody in the loo, just two old biddies, fiddling with their handbags. I went into a cubicle, pulled off my old jeans and shirt and slipped on my dress and shoes. When I came out, I finished off my make-up:

outlining and glossing my lips and, for a final touch, I stuck a tiny gold star on my cheek. I allowed myself one pose in front of the mottled mirror. Absolutely fabulous, darling. Divine!

I was giggling as the door opened and two girls I vaguely recognized walked in. They looked me up and down.

"You Goldie Moon?"

"Yes."

"Thought you would be," one of them said, as she put her bag down on the shelf.

"You're the singer, in the band, ain't yer?" the other one asked, as she chewed gum.

"Yes," I said.

"God, you're brave," she gushed.

I didn't know what to say, so I smiled and bent to pick up my bundle of clothes. A sock dropped out and I fumbled to retrieve it.

The girls turned to the mirror to brush their hair.

"Do ya know who's comin'?" the girl with the gum asked.

"Yeah . . . everybody," her friend replied.

I paused in the doorway, listening.

The girl with the gum chewed loudly for a moment and then said, "I heard the band's wicked. That Josh is supposed to be a brilliant guitarist."

I smiled, swung through the door and strode down the corridor back to the office. Three pairs of startled eyes looked up as I entered.

Josh whistled and stood up. "Yo, Goldie. You look real cool. Wicked. You the one, girl."

His eyes popped with admiration. I threw down my bundle of old clothes and gave a twirl, sending sparkling stars into the dim room. I wanted everybody's approval, but Josh's mattered most of all. I smiled at him, posed and pouted my lips.

He laughed. "You really somethin'," he said.

I fizzed with happiness and excitement and blew him a kiss. Then I caught Tiger's eye – cold, appraising. I felt a moment's doubt. Was the dress too much, too bright, too short? His lips puckered, the way they did when he was going to say something damning.

Josh leant in front of me and said to him. "Great, hey? Jus' what we need – bit of class. Impress the A & R man."

Tiger sniffed, then nodded slowly and said grudgingly, "She looks all right."

I sat down, thankful there wasn't going to be a scene. "Well, at least I've made an effort," I said. "You three look no different. Aren't you going to change?"

"It's not about what you wear," Tiger muttered.

"I brought somethin'," Josh said, reaching in his sports bag and unfolding a yellow T-shirt with a picture of Bob Marley on the front. "For good vibes," he said.

I smiled at him, watching as he pulled his faded orange T-shirt over his head. His body was lean and smooth, beautiful as burnished copper. As soon as he'd put the new shirt on, I reached over and smoothed the wrinkled shoulder seam, then rearranged his tangled dreadlocks – any excuse to touch him.

"How much longer before we go on," I asked.

"Zoë said she'd come and get us," Josh replied.

"Should have brought a book to read," Nazim moaned.

Josh leant back, folded his arms behind his head and said with a wry smile, "I spy with my beady eye, something beginning with 's'."

Nazim and I exchanged amused glances then made a few half-hearted suggestions, Tiger not deigning to join in. After Sellotape, shoes and stamps we gave up – it was only a small office. Nazim started saying silly things like "ceiling", "seventy-watt bulb" and "sausage-shaped pencil case".

Josh laughed, shaking his head, "No, no, no. Can't you see it?"

"No."

Josh raised his arms in the air and smiled broadly, his white teeth sparkling. "S for SUCCESS," he shouted.

Nazim and I laughed, but Tiger frowned and jumped to his feet.

"Where you goin'?" Josh asked.

"Anywhere, so long as I don't have to listen to you stupid nerds." And he shot out.

"What's wrong with him?" Nazim asked.

"Can't take the pressure," Josh said.

When he'd left we made up silly songs and planned what TV programmes we'd feature on. Nazim wanted *Top of the*

Pops, whilst Josh wanted more kudos from *Later with Jools Holland*. Then Tiger returned and told us that the hall was filling up fast.

"There's loads of old people and families . . . little kids. Hope they're not expecting some folk music or Radio Two stuff. Hope Zoë's made it clear that we're loud. I'm not toning it down for nobody."

Nazim got up and peered through the net curtain across the door. "Some kids from school going past . . . lot of 'em."

I joined him and looked closely through the net. My heart jumped as I saw faces I recognized but, thankfully, no Wes, no Ralph.

I was still staring at the door when it swung back and Zoë marched in.

"The hall's packed," she said. "I think we'd better start, some of them are getting restless. I've put some music on but they're all sitting waiting."

My stomach turned like a cement mixer. I felt sick. I wanted to pee.

"Zoë, I want to. . ."

But I was drowned out by loud clapping from hall, slow hand-claps building and feet stamping.

"Come on," Zoë said. "You're on."

CHAPTER TWENTY-ONE

We walked down the dim corridor to the back entrance of the stage. The others went to take up their positions whilst I waited in the wings. Lights glared in the smoky distance, but around me it was dark. My throat felt dry as chalk, I licked my lips and swallowed, struggling to get some saliva into my mouth.

The slow clapping stopped and there was a general buzz of expectant voices. I clenched and unclenched my fists, took a deep breath, concentrated.

There it was, the signal I'd been waiting for – a regular booming drum beat; strong, primitive. The crowd went quiet. I counted the beats. Thump, boom, slower than my heart. It went on echoing for a few seconds then it was joined by Josh's hard thrusting guitar. Still I waited. Tiger's explosive organ chords filled the air. I counted the bars. Tiger had told us a thousand times. "Hit 'em with sound. No standing at the mike saying, er . . . we are um . . . No Fear, twang, twang, and we, er . . . want to . . . er . . . if I can just get me guitar in tune now. . . None of that amateur stuff." So, I was ready to run on.

The sound was building – my moment arrived. Plunging

forward, I prayed I wouldn't trip on any loose wires. I stumbled against the PA amp, just missed stepping on a junction box, then ran headlong to the front of the stage and into the centre. When I grabbed the mike my hand was shaking so much I was amazed my voice worked at all. It sounded slightly strangled but after a few hoarse notes, I remembered what I'd been taught in the gospel choir. "Sing with your stomach not your throat." I took a deep breath and began to sing, hitting each note clean and true. There was a guitar break then a big chorus coming up and I knew if I managed that – I'd survive.

I heard Josh's guitar, the familiar riffs and remembered my cue. I sang the chorus, belting out the words. I couldn't hear myself; the instruments were drowning me. I just hoped it was carrying through OK on the mike.

Moving to the rhythm, I stamped and bent low, my voice raspy, guttural:

"You tell lies all your life
You hide from the truth
You pretend to your friends
But that ain't no proof
You are only alive if you walk your own walk
If you think your own thoughts
If you talk your own talk."

As the lights whirled I saw shadows, people out there listening, listening to me. The music seemed to die, I couldn't hear anything. For a moment everything stopped. Panic shook me, I put my hand over my eyes, tried to dip my head below the glare. Lights blasted my face, I heard a crash of cymbals, the whine of Josh's guitar, there was a lung-busting howl and I realized . . . it was coming from me. I was joined by Josh's high-octane guitar which broke into a lolloping riff and we were blasting. I sang like I was on fire and at the end of the number I stood, sweating but triumphant, as people clapped and cheered. Sashaying to the front, I bowed, then counted the bars into our next number – a stew of slow blues and funky guitar work. My eyes closed; I felt the rhythm.

And suddenly I stopped thinking. I was doing it like it was second nature. All the rehearsals Tiger had insisted on paid off. I was no longer consciously listening to the instruments; they were part of me. My voice was soaring, thrusting into the audience and I felt them responding. I leant forward, imagining I was singing to one special person out there. Smiling, I threw out my arms and danced. My red dress swung softly round my legs, the stars sparkling. I sang into the light and I loved it.

After two more fast numbers the audience applauded enthusiastically and I heard a few whistles. Then we slowed the tempo right down and I wrapped myself round the mike, singing into it real close. I unhooked it and went to the edge of the stage. Rows of heads, their features rubbed out by glare, were looking up at me. I stared wide-eyed trying to make out familiar faces. Mum, Dad, Patrick, Nancy, Zoë; they were all out there even though I couldn't see them.

Then, with a shiver of nerves, I wondered if the A & R man was amongst them, listening.

I missed my cue, was suspended in a haze of melting colours, until I heard someone shout, "Go for it Goldie!" I recognized Nancy's voice and smiled. It was OK. I was OK. I picked up the song and began to sing again, my voice flowing like a dark river.

The crowd were enjoying it, clapping and stamping after each number. I could tell we'd won them over, and when Josh sat down and began his acoustic set, they listened attentively, giving him respect. I slipped behind one of the amps, my heart swelling with pride as Josh played his songs, his voice soft and smoky, the lyrics melting from his soul.

When he'd finished I clapped till my hands tingled and there were shouts of more from the audience but Tiger cut in with some rapid techno. I sipped water, saw people get up and dance. A flower landed near my feet. I picked it up and stuck it in my hair.

Running forward again, I unhooked the mike from its stand and sang a few more up-tempo numbers, dancing to the beat. I grew more confident and, despite Tiger's warnings, I spoke to the audience between songs, introducing the band, then getting a bit carried away and telling them that No Fear was only a temporary name and we intended to change it.

"Suggestions on a postcard please to the Community Centre or Barnes Scrapyard," I said.

People began shouting out, suggesting names, so Tiger cut that short with a few frantic chords. I didn't care, I was fired up now and ready for anything. Turning to Josh, I mouthed "River Deep" at him, at the same time shimmying just like Tina Turner. Josh laughed and went into the unmistakable riff:

"Do I love you, my oh my?
River Deep, Mountain High...
Yeah, yeah, yeah..."

I'd studied the lyrics, I'd watched the videos and now I was Tina, taking short quick steps, flouncing, shaking my hips.

The audience went wild. Those old enough to remember it were joining in and the kids, who'd didn't know who the hell Tina Turner was, soon picked up the chorus. I bowed to rapturous applause then Josh started "Get Up, Stand Up".

The lights went up on the audience and I saw everybody clapping and singing along. I spotted Mum and Dad dancing in the aisle, Patrick bobbing up and down and Nancy gyrating like a hula hoop.

I scanned the rows of faces, wondering if I could spot the A & R man. I saw a few likely candidates and was pleased that they were all smiling. Everybody seemed to be enjoying themselves. I felt a giant wave of warmth rising to meet me – I was euphoric, bobbing on the tide. I ran to left and right, dancing and singing. Then as I returned to centre stage, something caught my eye. A pale shadow gliding through the dancers, dodging and weaving, out of sync with the rest of the crowd. A boy, tall and thin, white. My heart stopped as I recognized who it was – Andy Wragg. He was making his way over to the right-hand side of the hall and, behind him, his gang were sliding silently, intent on working their way through to the same spot. I followed their path and saw a group of black lads and, in their midst, was the bullet head of Wes Mabbott. Shit! What an idiot I was to think I'd kept him away.

Frantically, I kept singing. I did three more choruses of "Get Up, Stand Up". The gangs were closing in on each other; Tiger was yelling and waving his arms at me, wondering what the hell was going on.

The crowd hadn't noticed anything was wrong; they were swaying and singing loud enough to drown me. Sweat trickled down my arms and face.

I saw Wes brace himself, his head jut forwards, his shoulders tense. He'd spotted Andy Wragg. There were only a couple of metres between them – any moment now, someone would strike the first blow. I had to do something. Mum, Dad, Patrick, other mums and dads and kids were in the line of battle. Wes leant to one side, his hand went into his pocket. I saw the glint of a blade.

"Watch out!" I yelled into the mike. "He's got a knife."

The band stopped, the room froze into silence.

I waved my arms. "Wes, Andy – you don't wanna do this. Leave it."

I glared at the gangs, willing them to back away from one another. I held my breath. There was silence, nobody stirred. But then a swift, sudden movement came from Wes. He pushed two little kids out of the way and lunged at Andy Wragg. Next moment, a figure leapt past me, jumped off the stage and began to push his way through the crowd. It was Josh.

"Stay cool, Wes," he said softly. "Leave it."

The crowd parted, people watched open-mouthed. Wes's head jerked, then he turned and went for Josh. The crowd closed in, and I lost sight of what was happening. For a moment I couldn't see anything, panic blinding me. Then, I heard a shout and saw somebody hurtling forwards. A man grabbed Wes by the arms, pinning them firmly behind his back.

Wes yelled and thundered obscenities, but the man held on tight, dragging him to the back of the hall. Others joined in, hurling themselves on top of Wes and bustling him to the back exit.

Frantically, I scanned the crowd for Josh but I couldn't see him. A group of people were bending over and looking down at the floor. Josh was hurt, I knew it.

I wanted to run over to him but I couldn't move, my legs had turned to liquid and I was shivering violently.

"Josh, Josh," I couldn't even shout. I'd dropped the mike and my voice was just a whisper.

I saw Andy Wragg pushing through the crowd and my legs

burst into life. I lurched forward, springing off the stage. "Get him," I shouted, gesturing wildly.

Zoë caught me. "No, Goldie, stop."

"But he'll hurt somebody."

Zoë held my arms. "It's all right. You go to Josh."

I twisted round and looked over her shoulder just in time to see my Dad and another man dragging Andy Wragg out of the room.

"Dad," I called. "He'll get hurt."

Zoë shook her head. "No. The police are here – all over the place. I don't think we'll be seeing Wes Mabbott or Andy Wragg for a while."

She put her arms round me and I sagged against her. "Come on," she said, "Josh needs you."

CHAPTER TWENTY-TWO

Zoë guided me to Josh and when I saw him, sitting on the ground, blood dripping from his arm, I half-fell, half-knelt beside him.

"It's OK," he whispered. "He didn't get me too bad."

I leant my cheek against his as he dabbed at the wound with his T-shirt.

"See," he said, refolding the T-shirt to find a clean spot. "Told you Bob Marley give me good vibes. I could 'ave bin stabbed."

"You were," I said weakly.

All around us people were pushing and talking. "Is he all right?" "Did they get the attacker?" "Such a shame."

Zoë stood up and asked people to move away and, when we had a bit more space, she knelt down and examined Josh's arm. Somebody handed her a scarf and she tied it round the wound.

"There, that'll stop the bleeding. You were lucky. He could 'ave got a vein or somethin'. Good job he didn't. Wait there, I'll go and get the first-aid kit."

But Josh was getting to his feet. "I'm fine." he said. "Don't need no first aid. Let's get on down with the music."

Zoë looked at him closely. "You wanna carry on?"
Josh nodded. "Sure."
"I better go an' check with the police it's all right," Zoë said.

When she left, people started crowding in on us again; women reaching for Josh, trying to hug him or pat his back. From the other side of the room, somebody shouted, wanting to know what was going on. A girl at the front of the stage squealed. Noise swelled around us and I hung on to Josh, one arm round his shoulder and my other hand shielding his injured arm from the fray.

Josh grinned at me. "Be safer on stage," he said. "I'm gettin' mobbed."

Then the tall man who'd bundled Wes out of the room was back. He pushed his way through to us and clasped both of us in a wide embrace.

When he let go, the light caught his finely sculpted cheek bones, the wide forehead and long-lashed eyes, and I knew he was Josh's dad.

"You all right?" he asked, anxiously, his eyes searching Josh's face.

Josh nodded. "Yeah, just a scratch. We goin' on with the gig. Get the place buzzing. We not gonna let no losers stand in our way."

Then he turned to the people around us. "We were havin' a good time, yeah?"

"Yeah," everybody replied.

Josh grabbed me by the arm. "Then we gonna carry on groovin'," he said.

People made way for us as we walked back to the stage. Shouts and cheers followed us.

Tiger and Nazim came forward with bottles of water and Zoë appeared with plaster and scissors.

"It's OK," Zoë said. "The fuzz say it's cool for you to carry on. Keep the crowd entertained – defuse the situation."

She taped Josh's wound and peered closely at his face.

"Sure you OK?" she asked.

"Yeah," Josh said. "Come on, dudes, let's . . . deeefuse the situation."

He tied the bloodstained scarf around his head and picked up his guitar. A big cheer greeted him as he walked out under the stage lights.

Bare chested, a purple scarf trailing from his head, Josh fancied he was Jimi Hendrix and, with a big grin, went into the first shrieking riff of "Purple Haze". I smiled as the crowd applauded, then I stood back enthralled. Josh was magic. I'd never seen him play with such ferocity. He was savage, burning out his anger – almost ripping the strings from the frets.

I stood back, awe-struck and trembling, leaning against the amp. In the shriek of the ear-splitting chords I heard my voice echo, "He's got a knife". I shook my head to rid myself of the ghostly voice and then heard Josh, wild and shrill, "'Scuse me while I kiss the sky."

He was down on his knees playing like his life depended on it. I closed my eyes for a moment and saw Mabbott lunging towards him. I opened my eyes and hoped the police had got Wes and Wraggy; hoped they'd taken them away for ever.

My insides were rolling like they were seasick and, when Josh finished, I wondered if I'd be able to sing. But when I stepped into centre stage, I found it didn't really matter. The crowd were singing, our set list had gone to pot – it was party time.

Zoë appeared at my shoulder. "Come on. I wanna sing too," she shouted. "Let's do 'Get Up, Stand Up' again."

"You must be jokin'," I laughed.

Zoë giggled. "They'll think you're great whatever you do now." She grabbed hold of me and kissed my cheek. "You're a friggin' hero," she whispered.

"Thanks," I said.

Then I saw Tiger waving his arms and mouthing something at me.

"Dancing In the Street."

"What?" I asked, amazed.

I couldn't believe him. It was an old number. But he mouthed it again and began to play the intro looking right at me and smiling as everybody joined in. Any tension that remained ebbed away and people took up the rhythm and danced. When I stepped up to the mike, I saw Mum and Dad clapping along and beside them, Nancy laughing and bumping hips with Josh's dad.

The song went on for ever. Nobody wanted us to stop. As soon as I'd finished one chorus, people began to sing it again. I was going hoarse and the audience was deafening. Lights strafed the dancers, illuminating familiar faces. Suddenly, my stomach twisted in a nervous spasm – I'd spotted Ralph. But then I saw he was joining in, his bald head shining like a beacon, bobbing as he danced. And when the light swung back I saw more of the Mabbott mob dancing.

Wow! I could have whooped for joy. So much for solidarity.

Even when I saw Wraggy's mates standing with their arms folded silently watching, my happiness didn't disappear. They weren't singing but they didn't look about to strike. The music had won out, if only for tonight, and it was a start.

We played ourselves out with one of Josh's songs. As we bowed, the audience were still reluctant to let us go and were clapping and stamping for more, but Zoë signalled we had to wrap it up. The house lights went on and I saw crowds of happy faces looking up at me and then through the blur of faces all I saw for a moment was Mum and Dad, applauding for all they were worth.

In the blackness of backstage I paused, clenched my fists and heaved a big sigh. I couldn't believe we'd actually done it. All the rehearsals, all the arguments and worries were over. It had been a fantastic night, the music better than I could have hoped and the crowd loved us. I was tingling with success. Glowing with pride.

In the darkness, Josh came up behind me and put his good arm round my waist, kissing my neck.

"You were magic," he said.

I hugged him close and kissed him hard. "Thanks. You were pretty good yourself."

Tiger and Nazim joined us.

"OK, you two. There's not enough time for that," Tiger warned. "Let's go sign some autographs."

Laughing, we made our way to the office and had a few minutes to catch our breath before everybody started piling into the little room. Mum and Dad, smiling and shaking everybody's hands. Mum looking as if she'd won the lottery, kissing me, hugging Josh.

"It was brilliant," she said. "Thank God, everythin' turn out all right. Goldie, my child, you're a miracle and, Josh, you are somethin' else."

Soon the tiny office was so crowded that we couldn't move. Nazim's dad, looking proud and patting his son on the shoulder, Tiger's mum, placing her well-manicured hand tentatively on Tiger's arm, tears sparkling in her beautifully made-up eyes, and Nancy, smiling all over the place and hugging everybody, whilst friends pushed in at the door.

Then, suddenly, in front of me, was Josh's dad, his smile as dazzling as tropical sunshine.

"This is my dad – Michael," Josh said. "Dad, meet Goldie Moon."

He grasped my hand and I lit up inside.

"You were a star on that stage tonight," he said, smiling Josh's smile.

"Thank you," I muttered. "I was enjoying myself."

I couldn't take my eyes off him. Josh was so like him, the high, curving cheek bones, wide forehead, the little cleft in his chin, the lovely thick-lashed brown eyes. Josh put his arm round me and I looked from one to the other, lost for words. So many things were going through my head. I thought of Josh's mum and how sad it was she'd died, thought how lonely Josh's dad must have been, realized how precious Josh was to him and then shuddered when I thought of what could have happened to Josh.

I felt Josh stroke my shoulder and I looked up at him. "I thought you were badly hurt," I said.

Josh's dad took my hand. "He's fine. You did the right thing. You should be real proud of yourself."

I looked away. I didn't deserve praise. I should have spoken out sooner. I should have nailed Wes when I had the chance. Now he'd attacked Josh and it was my fault. That was something I had to face up to.

Then I caught what Josh's dad was saying. "Everybody knows Wes did it but no witnesses have come forward. He'll probably get a caution then he'll be free."

A sudden chill iced my veins. No, I couldn't let that

happen. Wes mustn't be set free, he'd nearly killed someone and tonight he'd been ready to finish the job.

I put down my glass and looked at Josh. "I've got to talk to the police, tell them what I saw."

Our eyes locked together. Josh looked thoughtful. He frowned and then nodded.

His dad leant forward and took hold of my hand. "Tomorrow will be soon enough. The police have Wes now and he ain't goin' nowhere in a hurry. You enjoy the rest of your night. Lots of people are waiting to congratulate you."

A look passed between him and Josh before he turned away.

"You told him, didn't you?" I asked Josh.

"Yeah. He's cool. I knew I could trust him and he knew you'd do the right thing in the end."

"Did you?" I asked.

He looked down at me, pursing his lips. "It's more complicated for me," he said.

"Why?" I asked.

"Because I don't want to lose you," he said.

There was a clinking of ice and glasses as Zoë produced a bottle of fizz. She popped the cork and, when everyone had a drink, she proposed a toast. "To No Fear. If they carry on as they've begun here tonight, then I predict major success."

People clapped and cheered and I began to relax and enjoy

myself, although I felt a bit uneasy when Zoë proposed another toast, this time just to Josh and me.

"To Josh and Goldie, our brave singer and guitarist, who both helped to avert a major crisis tonight and stopped anybody getting hurt," she said confidently, before remembering Josh's wound. "Except Josh, of course, but. . ."

"I'm OK," Josh shouted, waving his wounded arm.

When people had stopped cheering, Mrs Barnes proposed a toast to Josh's dad for grabbing Wes Mabbott, and to my dad for grabbing Andy Wragg. Then, Mr Barnes produced some real champagne and everybody was toasting everybody.

When Mum saw me downing a glass of champagne and stroking Josh's bare chest she hurried over and hauled me off to see Carlo and all the friends who'd come over from Blackheath.

"I'll see if I can find that boy a shirt," she said.

Carlo was waiting with a grin as wide as Tiger's keyboard. "You were brilliant, bowled me over," he said, giving me a major hug. "You really got the place jumpin'." He lifted me off my feet and twirled me round. "Your gran would have been so proud of you tonight," he whispered as he set me down.

"Thanks, Carlo," I said. Then I turned to my friends who started heaping praise on the band.

"You were mega, wicked! I couldn't stop dancin'. You should have seen Gemma, she was goin' wild."

"Wow! My ego's getting bigger by the minute," I protested.

Chola, my long-time friend from Blackheath, grimaced. "OK," she said, "Here's the rap. It was a good gig, you a wicked band but you need to take your fans in hand. Some of them got a weird way of showin' their appreciation of songs they knowin'. If they get to stabbin' you with knives, you gonna need a million lives."

I raised my eyebrows. "Thanks, Chola," I said, laughing. "I can always count on you to bring me down to earth."

When Josh joined us, I proudly introduced him to my friends and within moments they were talking like best buddies. Then Zoë rushed up to us.

"Here's somebody who wants to meet you," she said.

A small, rather scruffy-looking man, with a round face and a mop of curly black hair, shook my hand.

"Congratulations," he said. "Very promising. Distinctive voice. New stuff is good – raw, gritty. Yeah, very promisin'."

"Are you the A & R man?" I asked.

"Yeah. Dave Joseph. Margin records."

Tiger and Nazim joined us and we all shook hands.

I couldn't wait till the introductions stopped so I could ask the burning question. "Erm, so you thought we were . . . OK?"

Dave smiled. "Yeah, more than OK. I think you have a future."

Wow! I was speechless, knocked over by a tide of excitement. Some people whooped and Josh and I threw our arms round each other. Zoë was jumping up and down and I saw Chola and Carlo dancing. Then Tiger spoke up.

"We not making no deals, not till we've talked to our manager," he said.

For a moment everyone was silent, but then Josh said loudly and clearly. "Man, we ain't got no manager."

Everybody laughed except Tiger, who glared at Josh like he wanted to hit him.

Zoë put a calming hand on his arm and said soothingly, "Don't worry. Dave isn't a rip-off merchant. He's the real thing. An' you can't get better than Margin, can yer?"

"I know, I know," Tiger muttered. "But we not signing nothin'."

Dave nodded. "You're right to be cautious. But I'm not asking you to sign anything. I'm just the scout – I don't make the final decision. What we're talking about is a young band, a band with a lot of talent – one worth watchin'. We'll give you some studio time, maybe some development money. Then we'll see. It's a bit early to be talkin' deals."

He spoke seriously, glancing at Zoë. I figured he didn't want us to get any false ideas, imagine we were a dead cert for stardom, but my pulse was racing. I just kept thinking, we've got a chance, we're on our way.

When he left, he gave us his card and asked us to ring him to set a date for recording.

"Sure thing, man," Nazim said, pocketing the card.

"So we need a manager," Josh said, as the man disappeared. "A good one. Someone who'll look after our interests."

"Well, Zoë seems to have done a great job so far," I said.

There was a bit of discussion but nobody objected, and Zoë said she'd be delighted to take us on.

"Who knows where it might lead," she beamed.

We walked back to the office, arms round each other, bursting to relay the good news to our families. I was high, a mad smile plastered to my face, excitement bubbling up inside me like a fountain.

Congratulations flew round the room. Everybody talking, laughing and smiling. They were all there, Mum, Dad, Patrick, Nancy, Josh, Nazim, Tiger, Zoë, all the people who were so important to me.

I looked over at Josh; saw blood had seeped through the plaster on his arm and dried in a dark patch. I went over to him, but he was deep in conversation with my dad. I turned away and saw a shadow in the doorway.

"Can I come in?"

The red hair still startled me, and under it Miranda's face was flushed and anxious, the eyes glassy as marbles.

"You were very good," she said, her voice quiet, tentative.

I felt a stab of resentment that she'd dared show her face. This celebration was for friends.

She stepped forward. "I'm glad Josh is OK," she said.

"Yeah, so am I," I said.

She gave me a weak smile. "I 'eard about the man from the record company. 'Ope that goes fine."

"Thanks," I said shortly.

"Well, I'll be going then."

"Yes," I said.

She turned away and walked off down the corridor. I felt mean – I could have asked her to stay but seeing her had reminded me of things I'd rather forget.

I wandered out into the corridor and walked towards the stage. I needed to be alone.

Emerging from the dark wings into the glaring light, I blinked. The hall was empty, but in the stillness I sensed the stirring of warm bodies, the throbbing beat of music. Standing on the very edge of the stage I looked out over the rows of seats, imagining I heard again the shouts and applause of the crowd. I held out my arms and bowed, fingers crossed. I was hoping I'd be back on stage before long, hoping we'd do lots more concerts, hoping the band would go from strength to strength and our songs would make us famous. I touched one of the gold stars on my dress and wished that Josh and I would always be friends – and maybe more.

The stage lights were warm on my face and suddenly I caught the scent of flowers. Roses. I looked down and saw almost beneath my feet, a bouquet. I bent down to pick it up. The card read simply: "For Goldie".

Deep pink roses – Gran's favourite flowers. I buried my nose in their scent and I heard Gran's voice. It rang out clear and musical just as it always had.

"Listen, Golden Child, ain't no use walkin' if you walk in fear."

"I know, Gran," I said. I've kept quiet for too long. Sometimes you have to stand up and be counted. Tomorrow I'll do the right thing. Do what I should have done a long time ago. I'll go to the police and tell them what I saw on the night Andy Wragg was stabbed. It might make a difference.